*Samuel French Acting Edition*

# "But Why Bump Off Barnaby?"

## A Mystery-Farce in Three Acts

*by* Rick Abbot

SAMUELFRENCH.COM     SAMUELFRENCH.CO.UK

ISBN 978-0-573-60657-1

www.SamuelFrench.com
www.SamuelFrench.co.uk

---

### FOR PRODUCTION ENQUIRIES

#### UNITED STATES AND CANADA
Info@SamuelFrench.com
1-866-598-8449

#### UNITED KINGDOM AND EUROPE
Plays@SamuelFrench.co.uk
020-7255-4302

Each title is subject to availability from Samuel French, depending upon country of performance. Please be aware that *"BUT WHY BUMP OFF BARNABY?"* may not be licensed by Samuel French in your territory. Professional and amateur producers should contact the nearest Samuel French office or licensing partner to verify availability.

---

Please refer to page 104 for further copyright information.

## CAST OF CHARACTERS

(In order of appearance)

MEDKINS, a serenely capable butler
MAGNOLIA, a very apprehensive maid
ORION LEDUC, an arthritic British baronet
BARNABY FOLCEY, a poor relation of the Leducs
LADY BARBARA FENWICK, a rather deaf peeress
ROSALIND BARSTOW, a flamboyant fortune-hunter
CLEO BARTON, a middle-aged Hollywood actress
JEFF BARNETT, an intrepid police reporter
MISS BARNSDALE, an old nearsighted family governess
DORA DUNSTOCK, an adorable young dimwit

Time: The Present
Locale: The parlor of Marlgate, the
ancestral home of the Leducs


ACT ONE
A Friday evening just before sunset

ACT TWO
Very late that same night

ACT THREE
The next morning just before dawn

# "But Why Bump Off Barnaby?"

## ACT ONE

*Curtain rises on the parlor of Marlgate, ancestral home of the Leduc (luh-DEWK) family, somewhere in England. The room is elegant-but-gloomy—all gray stone and dark wood. Starting at lower left wall, we see a lightswitch that operates the room's two chandeliers, which hang high above centerstage right and left areas. Above this is an archway giving access to the front hallway and front door [unseen]. Just a step farther upstage we see the foot of a flight of stone stairs to the bedrooms, which curves out of sight behind a section of wall on which hangs a life-size—from waist upwards—painted cavalier, cloaked [the vertical overlap of the closed cloak is a real overlap of canvas, the resultant slot enabling a hand to come in and out as if one of the cavalier's own]; it hangs over a sideboard on which are many stemmed glasses, a small tray, and a decanter of sherry. Just above this, the wall angles sharply toward upstage center, and there is an access-archway to the cellar in it; dead-centered upstage is a large stone fireplace, hearth-level at waist-height, not at floor-level; over this hearth hangs a gold-framed portrait of grim-faced Great Grandfather Farlow. Then, mirror-image to the cellar-access, is the kitchen-access; mirror-image to the sideboard is a parson's bench against the wall [this rotates 180 degrees, on cue, and an identical parson's bench comes into view when it does so]; over the bench hangs any well-known work*

5

of art [*Mona Lisa, Blue Boy, American Gothic*—
something that the even-non-artistic audience-
members will know]; now, whenever the bench
rotates from Side #1 to Side #2, the painting over it
shows the rear view of its subject [this is silly, and it
is supposed to be; ours is not a very serious play].
Mirror-image to the front hall archway are french
doors leading to a garden [unseen]; between the
bench and these doors hangs a bell-pull, the sort
used to summon servants. Below these doors, mirror-
image to the lightswitch, a writing-desk and its chair
is against the wall; the telephone on this desk is the
old-fashioned kind with mouthpiece on a stand, and
earpiece on a hook. Just downstage of the hearth,
matching settees face a rather large table [the table is
unusual in that its floor-to-tabletop cloth hangs on
only two sides—but apparently on the upstage-side,
too, thanks to 90-degree-angled mirrors (see Set Design Diagram)—so that the audience has what seems
to be a clear view of the entire under-table area, but
actually cannot see the upstage quarter, this area
henceforth to be known as the "cubbyhole"].

At curtain-rise, it is early evening, and plenty of light
comes in via the garden doors, which are open.
Chandelier-lights are out. MEDKINS the butler is
onstage at the sideboard, and MAGNOLIA the maid
wields a featherduster at the writing-desk; their
livery tells us at once what they are, job-wise. As
soon as curtain has opened fully, MEDKINS ceases fid-
dling with the sideboard-top items, and turns to look
toward MAGNOLIA, who is doing her dusting with a
definite lack of enthusiasm. She is young and pretty;
he is not so young and not so pretty. He watches her
a moment, clears his throat loudly, and she reacts
and glances his way, not very amiably.

MAGNOLIA. *Now* what's stuck in your craw?!

MEDKINS. That is no way to address a butler!

MAGNOLIA. Well, that's no way to stare at a hard-working maid!

MEDKINS. Magnolia, haven't you finished *yet*? They'll *be* here at any moment!

MAGNOLIA. (*Nervously.* [*As she speaks nearly* all *her lines.*]) I'm sorry, Mr. Medkins, really I am. This part of the old mansion hasn't been *opened* in so long there's dust on nearly *everything*! Even in the drawers!

MEDKINS. (*Will move to fireplace, take one of a tube of long wooden fireplace-matches there, strike it, and start the fire up* [*NOTE: This is a fake fire, one of those electric "glow-log" fires, and whenever room lights go out,* it *will go out, too, for the same duration; this is just as ridiculous as that rear-of-portrait-duplicate over parson's bench, but it is supposed to be that way.*], *during his speech:*) Well, hurry it up, girl, hurry it up! Mr. Leduc was quite specific about the time his guests were due to arrive. It wouldn't do to have them all raising dust-clouds with every step they took!

MAGNOLIA. (*Dusting the desk a bit faster.*) This old feather-thing doesn't do much good. It just moves the dust to a different place. I do wish the old mansion had a vacuum-cleaner.

MEDKINS. And where would you plug it in if we *had* one? We're lucky the Master electrified the *ceiling*-lights in this creaky old place. It could get terribly tiresome hand-lighting chandeliers full of wax candles!

MAGNOLIA. (*Leaves desk, moves nearer downstage center.*) At least candles don't go out during a thunderstorm! (*Shivers and looks about.*) I'd hate to find myself here during unexpected blackness!

MEDKINS. (*Moving upstage of left settee toward hall archway.*) You're not likely to find yourself here much *longer* if you keep on shirking your *duties*, Magnolia!

MAGNOLIA. (*Now downstage of table.*) Do you know . . . I'd almost *enjoy* getting the sack from this place! I had such trouble sleeping last night—with all those strange noises . . . !

MEDKINS. (*Pauses at archway, turns to face her.*) You're imagining things. There are no noises here at night. Oh, perhaps a squeaky floorboard or two. But *I* had no trouble sleeping at all.

MAGNOLIA. That's because you're not a helpless young girl. Creatures that come creeping through the night almost *never* bother about butlers.

MEDKINS. My dear girl, I *do* hope you won't talk that way in front of the *guests*?

MAGNOLIA. I won't have to. They'll know. Ten minutes in this dreadful pile of ancient stones, and they'll know. It's in the very walls, it is! A kind of cold, queasy feeling that comes with the dampness of the place, and penetrates to your very bones!

ORION. (*Off.*) Here, now, what's this, what's all this?! (ORION LEDUC *descends stairs into view; he is well dressed, well over middle age, and more than a bit pompous of manner; arthritic knees make him short-step rapidly, like a geisha.*)

MEDKINS. (*To* MAGNOLIA.) *Now* you're for it, girl! (*Assumes deferential attitude as* ORION *reaches parlor level.*) Good evening, sir.

ORION. Never mind the amenities, Medkins! What's this fool girl been blathering about now?!

MAGNOLIA. (*With a half-hearted curtsey.*) I *do* beg your pardon, Mr. Leduc, sir. I'm just not *used* to working in such a large spooky place. When the agency sent me over, nobody told me—

ORION. "Spooky"?! How dare you! Marlgate Manor has been in my family for countless generations!

MAGNOLIA. All right, then—*old* and spooky! Give me the sack if you like, but it won't alter the facts!

ORION. Now, see here, young lady—! (*DOOR CHIMES—which are loud and sonorous, almost like the sound of large brass gongs—sound, and distract him.*) Oh, blast! The guests are here! Medkins—?

MEDKINS. (*With a slight bow.*) At once, sir. (*Turns and exits toward front door.*)

ORION. As for you, young lady, you can thank heaven the guests arrived so opportunely for you. There's no time to hire a new girl, now!

MAGNOLIA. If you could get one! (*He opens his mouth to retort, but she is already heading toward kitchen on her line:*) I'll just go see about the horse's doovers!

ORION. (*As she exits.*) That's "*hors d'oeuvre*"—! (*But she is gone, and he just has time to regain his decorum before* BARNABY FOLCEY *enters via archway,* MEDKINS *following.*)

BARNABY. Uncle Orion, as I live and breathe! You haven't altered in twenty years!

ORION. (*Uncertainly, as* BARNABY *pumps his hand vigorously.*) I'm afraid you have the advantage of me, sir—?

BARNABY. It's Barnaby, Uncle! Barnaby Folcey! Have *I* changed so much, then? (*Stops handshaking.*)

ORION. Barnaby! Of course! Now I recognize you! Of course, you were a mere lad in school when I last saw you—and you certainly didn't have those muttonchop sidewhiskers or that mustache!

BARNABY. (*With a rueful headshake.*) That's true enough, I daresay. Where do the years go to, eh?!

ORION. Where, indeed! Where, indeed! Ah, but it's splendid having you home again after all these years. How was your trip?

BARNABY. A bit rough halfway over, but otherwise quite pleasant. It was good of you to send me the plane ticket. It's not easy being the poorest member of an otherwise wealthy family.

MEDKINS. (*Who has been busying himself at sideboard since his return, now approaches with two stemglasses of wine on a small tray.*) Some sherry, Mr. Folcey? . . . Mr. Leduc?

ORION. (*Taking his.*) Splendid idea! The evenings are growing a bit chilly.

BARNABY. (*Taking his.*) And arriving earlier, too. Thank you, Medkins.

ORION. It *is* getting a bit dim in here at that! Medkins—?

MEDKINS. At once, sir. (*Moves, tray still in hand, to lightswitch, and flips it on; LIGHTS COME UP FULL [and chandeliers go on]; from here on, LIGHT THROUGH GARDEN DOORS WILL DIM TO BLACKNESS OVER NEXT FIVE MINUTES OR SO.*)

ORION. Ah, that's much better! Come along, Barnaby, let's have our sherry over by the fire. (*He will move that way, BARNABY following, and they will sit opposite one another at upstage ends of the two settees, during:*)

MEDKINS. (*Returning tray to sideboard.*) Will there be anything else, sir?

ORION. Not at the moment, Medkins, thank you. Just stay on the alert for the arrival of the rest of my guests.

MEDKINS. As you wish, sir. (*Will move from sideboard and exit into front hall.*)

BARNABY. Must be wonderful having servants. Just say the word, and a thing is done. How long has Medkins been with you?

ORION. Well—as a matter of fact—it's most embarrassing to admit, but—I only hired him for the duration of the houseparty. And a young snip of a maid, named Magnolia. They both arrived yesterday morning.

BARNABY. Oh? I had thought—?

ORION. You see, my boy, it's the blasted taxes. No one runs a mansion as it was done in the old days. Can't afford it, do you see? Servants are hard to come by—*good* servants nearly *impossible* to come by—and in either case, they're beastly expensive to have around.

BARNABY. But how do you manage such a large place without them?

ORION. Oh, I don't. Only opened this wing for the party. Actually, I live in just a few small rooms in the other wing, normally. Don't really *need* a domestic staff for anything *that* size, now do I!

(*Over next two speeches,* LADY BARBARA FENWICK, *a tall, matriarchal type in a long gown and cumbersome jeweled necklace, will descend stairs into room.*)

BARNABY. No, I suppose not. Though I had thought the Leduc family was absolutely *rolling* in money.

ORION. Afraid not, afraid not. A paltry few million pounds, is all. And when that's gone—! (*Shrugs, then see* BARBARA *and rises.*) Ah, here's my sister-in-law!

BARNABY. (*Also rising.*) Your late brother's widow—? Oh, of course! Lady Barbara Fenwick, is it not?

BARBARA. (*Moving toward them, upstage of settees.*) Orion, aren't you going to introduce me?

ORION. Barbara, this is your nephew-in-law, Barnaby Folcey, from the United States.

BARBARA. (*Takes* BARNABY'S *hand briefly.*) Happy to meet you, Mr. Tate.

BARNABY. "Folcey," Lady Barbara.

BARBARA. Now, now, you mustn't flatter me!

ORION. (*When* BARNABY *flashes him a bewildered look.*) She's deaf as a post. Should have warned you. Hardly ever catches a word of a conversation.

BARBARA. (*To* BARNABY.) Oh, really? I have many friends there.

BARNABY. (*At sea.*) *Where*?

BARBARA. Why, at Conover Station, of course. How long have you lived there?

ORION. Barbara, I didn't say "Conover Station," I said "conversation"!

BARBARA. Yes, but how *long* has he lived there?

BARNABY. (*Gives it up.*) Oh, ever so long!

BARBARA. What do you mean, "so long"? You're not leaving *already*?

ORION. (*Before things can get out of hand.*) Barbara, we were just having some sherry. Would you like a glass?

BARBARA. (*Brightening.*) Mrs. Michaels' class! Of course! *That's* where I know him from! (*To* BARNABY.) It was *such* fun, wasn't it! The bright lights, the applause—!

BARNABY. (*To* ORION, *haplessly.*) Uh . . .

ORION. No-no, Barbara, he has nothing to do with your amateur theatricals! This is Barnaby Folcey, my only boy's brother! (*Sees* BARNABY *is staring at him in astonishment, corrects:*) I mean—my only brother's boy! Your brother-in-law's son!

BARBARA. (*Takes* BARNABY'S *hand.*) Happy to meet you, Mr. Lawson! I never *did* catch your name when we were in Acting School together!

BARNABY. Really, Lady Barbara—!

ORION. It's no use, Barnaby. Once she gets a wrong notion in her head, there is no disabusing her of it. From now on, she will insist you two met while sharing a class!

BARBARA. Sherry in a glass? What *else* would I drink it from?! (*Moves toward sideboard, where she will pour herself some.*)

ORION. That's one nice thing about Barbara—sooner or later, the proper message gets through. In a roundabout way, of course. (*DOOR CHIMES sound.*) Ah! More guests! Capital, capital! (*He and* BARNABY *move downstage of table, looking toward hall.*)

MEDKINS. (*Steps just inside room from hall to announce:*) Miss Rosalind Barstow!

ORION. (*Horrified.*) *What*?! (*Then he stares in shock as* ROSALIND BARSTOW, *a svelte and elegantly gowned woman in her mid-30s, sweeps into the room and heads directly for* ORION, *hands outstretched toward him.*)

ROSALIND. Orion, *dar*-ling! I heard you were having a party, and I just *couldn't* stay away!

ORION. Damn and blast, Rosalind, this is a *family* gathering!

ROSALIND. (*Coyly-but-possessively links her arm in his.*) But Orion, my sweet, I'm *practically* a member of your family, aren't I? I mean, it's *only* a matter of *time* . . . !

ORION. (*Gives nervous, embarrassed laugh, then notices* BARNABY *staring at* ROSALIND *in curiosity, and says reluctantly:*) Miss Rosalind Barstow—my nephew, Barnaby Folcey. Rosalind is—uh—a *friend* . . .

BARNABY. (*Hazarding a polite guess.*) . . . Former schoolmate?

ORION. Well, *hardly,* Barnaby! Dash it all, I'm old enough to be her—

ROSALIND. (*With no interval between his last word and hers:*) Husband.

(ORION *bridles and glares at her; she simply smiles sweetly; then DOOR CHIMES sound, and* MEDKINS *exits to hall, and she releases arms with* ORION, *and* MAGNOLIA *enters from kitchen with trayful of* hors d'oeuvre *and moves toward sideboard.*)

MAGNOLIA. Here's the horse's doovers. Get 'em while they're hot! (*Sets tray on sideboard as* ORION *winces at her line.*)

ORION. Magnolia, *must* you?!

MAGNOLIA. Must I *what*, sir?

ORION. Oh, never mind, never mind! Just—go into the hall and see about taking the guests' baggage upstairs!

MAGNOLIA. That's housemaid-work. I was hired as a party-maid!

ORION. (*Through grating teeth.*) We may move the party *upstairs*! Now, get *to* it!

(MAGNOLIA *jumps in fear and scurries off to hall, barely missing a collision with* MEDKINS, *who enters as before, takes a stance, and speaks:*)

MEDKINS. Miss Cleo Barton and—friend.

ROSALIND. I say! Not *the* Cleo Barton? The Hollywood movie star?

BARNABY. (*Brightening.*) Oh, really?

(*Then all conjecture is academic as* CLEO BARTON, *gowned and coifed—and minked, if possible—like a typical Hollywood glamor girl, enters the room, arm-in-arm with* JEFF BARNETT, *a handsome young man in his probable mid-20s;* CLEO *could almost pass for mid-20s herself, if the lighting were right, but is probably at least ten years older than* JEFF; *she pauses—*JEFF *pausing with her—just inside room.*)

CLEO. Orion! And Lady Barbara! It's been simply ages and ages!

BARBARA. (*Who has been listening—well, trying to listen—to various speeches since she went to sideboard for sherry, sort of "hovering on the fringe" of events, peers uncertainly at* CLEO.) Orion, isn't that Cleo Barton?

ORION. That's what Medkins *said*, my dear.

BARBARA. What *about* Medkins' head?

(*But* CLEO—*used to* BARBARA—*ignores this, and goes directly to* ORION, *with* JEFF *trailing after her.*)

CLEO. (*Kissing him briefly on the cheek.*) It's been such a long, dreary ride up here—isn't anyone going to offer us a drink?

BARBARA. It must have been a long, dreary ride up here—isn't anyone going to offer them a drink?

ORION. (*Sees* JEFF'S *bewildered reaction to this.*) You'll have to pardon my sister-in-law—

MAGNOLIA. (*Enters from hall.*) She's deaf as a post.

ORION. Magnolia!

MAGNOLIA. You told me so yourself!

ORION. (*Gives it up, turns back to* JEFF.) Hard to get competent help anymore, Mister—uh—?

CLEO. Oh, how stupid of me! Orion, darling, I'd like you—(*a bit louder, to rest of gathering.*) I'd like *all* of you—to meet one of my oldest, closest and dearest friends: Jeff . . . uh . . . ?

JEFF. "Barnett."

CLEO. Barnett.

JEFF. Actually, we just met tonight.

CLEO. (*Quickly.*) But some friendships seem as if they'd gone on forever, you know! From the moment I saw him, I just *knew* we had much in common!

JEFF. We met in a bar.

CLEO. "Pub," Jeffrey, "pub"! (*To* OTHERS.) Mr. Barnett is an American.

BARBARA. Cleo, aren't you going to introduce your young man?

MAGNOLIA. See? Deaf as a post.

ORION. Magnolia! I thought I told you to see to the baggage!

MAGNOLIA. There are six suitcases. I can't carry more than two.

ORION. Then make *three trips*!

MAGNOLIA. But I don't even know which *rooms* they're supposed to be in!

ROSALIND. Which room is closest to Mr. Leduc's?

ORION. Rosalind! You brought baggage?! You weren't even invited to the *house*, let alone into the *bedrooms*!

ROSALIND. (*Chucks him under the chin, fondly.*) But it's only a matter of time!

MEDKINS. (*Since his last speech has gone to sideboard and filled stemglasses for* CLEO, JEFF, ROSALIND, *placed them on a small tray, and has now moved down toward group below table.*) Sherry, Miss Barton? . . . Miss Barstow? . . . Mr. Barnett?

(EACH *ad-libs some form of thanks and takes a glass, both* MEDKINS' *offers and their acceptances done in lowered voices, almost as background sound, during next two speeches:*)

ORION. (*Has moved near* MAGNOLIA.) Now, it's very simple, my girl—place Miss Barstow's things in the Blue Room, Miss Barton's in the Green Room, Mr. Folcey's in the Grey Room—

MAGNOLIA. But how do I know which bags are which?!

JEFF. (*Has his sherry, now, and has overheard them.*) Oh, listen, why don't we all carry our *own* bags upstairs? It would simplify things enormously.

MAGNOLIA. That's a *marvelous* idea! (*Curtseys and exits toward kitchen before* ORION *can explode.*)

ORION. (*Staring after her.*) That girl! If servants weren't so *beastly* hard to get *hold* of—!

ROSALIND. *Shame* on you, Orion!

ORION. (*Turns to face her, stiffly proper.*) I *mean* so beastly hard to get from an *agency*! (*Then belatedly remembers something, turns to* JEFF.) I say—did you just say—"carry our own bags upstairs"? That is to say—do you mean—*you've* brought overnight things, too?

CLEO. Really, darling, he can't go the entire weekend without a change of underclothing!

ORION. What? Oh! Of course not, naturally! But— that is—when you said you'd met him in a pub, I naturally thought—I mean—he just happened to have his *baggage* with him?

JEFF. Well, actually, it was more of an *inn*. I was at the bar, trying to get a room for the night, but they were all booked up, so—

CLEO. So *I* told him I knew an absolutely *divine* place where he could spend the night, and it wouldn't cost him a shilling!

ORION. (*Glumly defeated.*) Meaning *here*?

CLEO. Why, where *else*, darling? It's not as though you didn't have the space. And it's getting far too late for him to find lodgings elsewhere . . . so—?

ORION. Cleo, I was *not* planning on *evicting* the gentleman! I was merely taken unawares to learn that—

(*DOOR CHIMES sound.*)

ROSALIND. More guests? How cozy! (MEDKINS *exits to front door, during:*) Do you have enough beds to go around?

ORION. I'm not certain. We may have to double up.

ROSALIND. (*As if scandalized.*) But think of my *reputation*!

CLEO. (*Cattily.*) Perhaps *that's* what *decided* him!

(ROSALIND *bridles.*)

BARNABY. Perhaps some of us might stay at the inn.

CLEO. Nonsense! *I* certainly don't mind sharing a room!

Rosalind. (*Sweetly.*) She's probably got affadavits!

(Cleo *bridles.*)

Jeff. (*Feeling guilty about being uninvited.*) *Seriously,* if unexpected arrivals are crowding you—

Rosalind. Mr. Barnett, I'm sure Cleo was *quite* serious.

Jeff. But, as an uninvited guest, if I'm causing a problem—

Rosalind. Don't give Orion ideas—I'm an uninvited guest myself!

Barbara. Was that the doorbell?

Barnaby. (*To* Orion.) I see what you mean. Sooner or later—

Orion. (*Nods.*)—she catches up with events.

(Medkins *enters, followed by* Miss Barnsdale ["Barnsy"], *a bifocaled ancient in a once-elegant-now-faded gown.*)

Medkins. Miss Barnsdale!

Magnolia. (*Just entering from kitchen, stops and reacts.*) Oh, dear, not *another* bag!

Barnsy. I *beg* your pardon?!

Medkins. (*Quickly.*) I believe Magnolia was referring to the increase in *luggage,* Miss.

Magnolia. As if I didn't have *enough* of it to carry up them stairs!

Orion. Which reminds me, Magnolia—hadn't you better get started?

Magnolia. Oh, damn and blast! (*She will head for hall and exit [NOTE: From this point, "*Magnolia UP*" will mean that she enters from hall with two pieces of luggage and vanishes upstairs; "*Magnolia DOWN*"* *will mean that she descends minus bags and exits to hall for her next load.*])

ORION. (*The moment* MAGNOLIA *has crossed past the newcomer.*) Come in, Barnsy, come in! You look a bit chilly.

BARNSY. (*Moves toward hearth; she does not* quite *grope her way, but we can see that her vision is not all it should be.*) Yes, I am. I believe there is a storm brewing outside.

CLEO. Oh, drat! I just had the Bentley waxed and polished! Are you sure?

BARNSY. (*Warming her hands at the hearth.*) Well, the sky was filled with absolutely *threatening* clouds as I strolled up here from the cottage.

(MAGNOLIA *UP.*)

JEFF. The cottage?

ORION. Oh, dash it all, I completely forgot you two hadn't met! Barnsy is a retired member of the house staff—she was my grandniece Dora's governess. She uses the small cottage at the foot of the estate.

BARNSY. Orion, it is considered proper manners for the gentleman to be introduced to the lady first—*then* the lady to the gentleman!

ORION. Oops, sorry! (*To* JEFF.) If you haven't guessed, Miss Barnsdale was *my* governess, too! (*To* BARNSY.) This is Jeffrey Barnett.

BARNSY. That's all you're going to tell me about him?

ORION. That's all I *know*!

ROSALIND. Cleo picked him up in a pub.

JEFF. That's not as bad as it sounds, Miss Barnsdale.

BARNSY. You mean it's worse? How delicious!

(MAGNOLIA *DOWN.*)

BARBARA. You mustn't say "Howdy"—even if he *is* an American.

CLEO. Why, Lady Barbara, you must be improving! However did you learn his nationality?

BARBARA. (*Cups hand behind one ear.*) He's gnashing *what?*

ROSALIND. So much for her improvement.

CLEO. But really, Rosalind, how *did* she know the nationality?

JEFF. Maybe it was a lucky guess. The cut of my clothes, or something?

(MAGNOLIA *UP.*)

BARBARA. (*To* JEFF.) Your pictures don't do you justice, young man.

BARNSY. *What* pictures?

CLEO. Ah! I think I've got it! Jeff came in with me, and Lady Barbara imagines he must be another American movie star!

(*From garden, there comes a loud RUMBLE OF THUNDER.*)

BARNABY. (*Moves toward garden doors.*) I think Barnsy may be right—there *is* a storm brewing out there!

CLEO. Shouldn't we shut the garden doors?

ORION. No need, no need—there's a considerable overhang of the house just above the terrace there—no danger of the rain coming in—besides, a good downpour would freshen the air in here—old unused rooms *do* get a bit musty.

ROSALIND. I've never *seen* this part of the house, Orion—won't you give me a tour of the premises?

BARNSY. Certainly not now, Rosalind—perhaps after

the rest of the party has arrived. It wouldn't be good manners for him to leave his guests.

ORION. Never argue deportment with Barnsy. She's quite right. Besides, I must be here when we're all gathered together to make my announcement.

BARNABY. (*Has been looking out into night, now turns back.*) Announcement, Uncle?

CLEO. Aha! I *thought* there might be an ulterior motive for this gathering!

(MAGNOLIA *DOWN.*)

ROSALIND. But this is totally fascinating! How mysterious it all sounds!

JEFF. Just how many more are you expecting, Mr. Leduc?

ORION. Oh, just one more—my grandniece Dora—then our party will be complete.

(*DOOR CHIMES SOUND;* MEDKINS *exits to hall.*)

CLEO. Perhaps *that's* her!

BARNSY. Perhaps that's *she!*

CLEO. Oh, come off it, Barnsy. You're not in the classroom now!

ORION. (*Calls hallward.*) Medkins? Is that Dora?

MEDKINS. (*Enters, with folded newspaper.*) Sorry, sir, but it was only the paperboy. (*Will place newspaper at lower end of sideboard, during:*)

JEFF. Your paperboy rings the bell and hand-delivers the news?

(MAGNOLIA *UP.*)

BARNABY. He can hardly toss it onto the lawn from the road—it's nearly a half-mile down the driveway.

ORION. Dear me, I wonder what *is* delaying Dora? Not like her to be tardy.

BARNSY. Of course, she has quite a long distance to come.

ROSALIND. Didn't she settle someplace in America?

ORION. Dover.

CLEO. Oh? I could have sworn—

BARNSY. He doesn't mean the white cliffs, he means the *other* one.

BARNABY. *What* other one?

JEFF. In Delaware. It's the capital city.

ORION. I say! How did you know *that*?

JEFF. The capital of Delaware is hardly secret information, Mr. Leduc.

ORION. I mean that my grandniece *settled* there. How did you know that?

JEFF. Why—you just *told* me.

CLEO. Orion, darling, stop being so jumpy! It was a perfectly obvious conclusion.

ORION. Oh. Yes, yes. I daresay it was.

BARNSY. How long ago *did* dear little Dora emigrate to America? It seems ages.

ORION. Oh, years, and years—she was a mere child at the time—I don't suppose she'll remember any of us— except perhaps Barnsy—teachers seem to stick with one, for some reason. The rest of us will all undoubtedly seem like strangers to her.

ROSALIND. You're forgetting—I *am* a stranger to her—and so is Jeffrey, here.

BARNSY. But not Barnaby. I'm *sure* she won't have forgotten *him*!

BARNABY. Oh? Why should she particularly remember *me*?

ORION. Barnaby, dear fellow, you surely remember how you used to take her riding piggyback all over the estate—a child doesn't forget things like that. She'll know your face in a minute.

CLEO. Not if he took her piggyback, Orion. But she should certainly be able to recognize the back of his head.

(MAGNOLIA *DOWN*.)

MEDKINS. I beg your pardon, Mr. Leduc, but I think I should tell you that it is nearly time for dinner to be served.

ORION. What? It can't be!

MEDKINS. You *did* say at eight-thirty sharp, sir.

ORION. Where *does* the time go to! Well, if we must, we must—!

BARNSY. But surely we won't start without dear little Dora, Orion?

CLEO. I don't see why not! If she chooses to arrive late, let *her* be the one to eat her dinner cold.

ROSALIND. Though it pains me to say it, I agree with Cleo.

ORION. Oh, very well, then, we'll all go in to dinner *now*.

(MAGNOLIA *enters from hall with pair of suitcases, but has only gotten to foot of stairs when she stops for:*)

MEDKINS. Better leave those right there, Magnolia, it's time to start serving dinner.

JEFF. (*As she sets bags downstage of sideboard.*) Oh, those are mine—I'll just take them upstairs myself. (*While moving to do so:*) Any particular room, Mr. Leduc?

ORION. The—um—the Gold Room should be ready for occupancy, I believe.

MEDKINS. That would be the fourth door to your right at the head of the stairs, sir.

BARNABY. (*As* JEFF *starts to pick up bags.*) Here, those look heavy. Let me give you a hand.

MAGNOLIA. (*As he moves toward* JEFF.) Where were you when *I* needed help?!

ORION. Really, Magnolia!

JEFF. (*As* BARNABY *takes one of the bags.*) Thank you, Barnaby.

(JEFF *and* BARNABY *will exit upstairs with bags at the same time* MEDKINS *and* MAGNOLIA *exit hallward—which is the way to get to the diningroom on the far side of the hall.*)

BARBARA. (*Setting her emptied glass down on sideboard.*) That sherry's given me an appetite. Isn't it dinnertime yet?

CLEO. (*Exasperated.*) Perhaps we should all write our remarks down on idiot-cards and *show* them to the old girl!

BARBARA. Cards? Before dinner? Perhaps *afterwards, my dear*—that is, if everyone likes to play bridge . . .

ORION. Will someone kindly take her by the arm and lead her to the table? I'm not up to explaining things to her in words.

ROSALIND. (*Moving to do so.*) I hope she doesn't think she's being kidnaped!

BARBARA. (*As* ROSALIND *leads her off toward dining room.*) Oh, I've already had my nap, dear.

ORION. (*Offers* CLEO *his arm.*) Shall we then, my dear?

BARNSY. (*Hurt and annoyed.*) I suppose *I* can just walk in to dinner *unescorted*!

ORION. (*Just as annoyed.*) Oh, don't be a social fussbudget, Barnsy! (*Extends his other arm, which she takes, slightly mollified.*) Come along, old girl, come along!

(ORION, BARNSY *and* CLEO *will exit diningroomward during:*)

BARNSY. What are we *having* for dinner, Orion?

ORION. Oh, the usual fare—boiled mutton, Yorkshire pudding, and gooseberry trifle.

CLEO. (*With a notable lack of anticipation.*) And they call *America* the home of the brave!

(*As they exit, there is a faint FLICKER OF LIGHT-NING outside garden doors, followed by a MILD RUMBLE OF THUNDER; then, a short moment later:*)

DORA. (*Off.*) Yoo-hoo! Anybody home? (*Enters from garden, wearing a topcoat, and carrying two small suit-cases; she is a girl barely out of her teens, strikingly pret-ty, and her voice is always sparkling and bright, which is more than we can say for her brain; she looks about empty room, poised on the inner threshold, then sets her bags down before desk, and removes her topcoat; as she turns her back to the room while laying topcoat across back of desk chair,* JEFF *comes trotting down stairs, sees her, and halts at foot of stairs, looking ill-at-ease.*)

JEFF. (*After a moment.*) Hello, Dora.

DORA. (*Turns, reacts.*) Jeff! What in the world are *you* doing here?! (*Moves in his direction, and he in hers, and they will meet just below table, during:*)

JEFF. I guess I owe you some sort of explanation—

DORA. Yes, you most certainly do! Why, when we said goodbye at the airport, I very definitely told you you were *not* to interfere, in any way, with—

JEFF. But I was so worried about you! And your great-uncle's cablegram was so mysterious—!

(*They have met and stopped, now, and he takes her hands, and as he does so,* BARNABY *descends stairs, sees them, and stops.*)

BARNABY. Another guest? I didn't hear the door-chimes—?

DORA. I came in through the garden. It was such a lovely night, I decided to walk across the fields from the station.

JEFF. Lovely night? It's damp and chilly and threatening to rain!

DORA. (*Rapturously.*) That's what I love about England! You can always rely on the weather.

BARNABY. (*Moving down to join them.*) I don't believe I've had the pleasure—?

DORA. Oh, British weather's never a pleasure. But it's so typical!

BARNABY. I mean, we haven't met—have we?

JEFF. Oh, sorry. Let me do the honors. Barnaby Folcey—Dora Dunstock.

DORA. (*In the act of taking* BARNABY'S *hand.*) Do you know—I used to have a relative by that name! "Barnaby Folcey," I mean, not "Dora Dunstock." *I'm* Dora Dunstock.

JEFF. Dora, I'm *sure* Barnaby knows which of you is which.

BARNABY. Dora! How delightful to see you again!

DORA. Again?

JEFF. Darling, Barnaby *is* that relative of yours!

DORA. He can't be! Barnaby was ever so much taller! He used to take me piggyback all over the estate.

BARNABY. Dora, you were barely three years old at the time. *Naturally* I was taller then!

DORA. How much taller *were* you? You can't have *shrunk*?

JEFF. Of course not, darling. But *you've grown*!

DORA. Oh! *That* must be it! But why don't I recognize your whiskers?

BARNABY. I didn't *have* them then. Wasn't much more than a young lad *myself*!

DORA. What do you mean, "yourself"? *I* certainly wasn't a young lad.

JEFF. Really, darling, let's not pursue the matter.

BARNABY. I say! That's the third time you've called her that.

DORA. Called me what?

BARNABY. "Darling"!

DORA. (*Takes a backstep.*) How dare you! I hardly know you!

JEFF. Dora, Barnaby was merely quoting *me*! He wondered how *I* could call you "darling" on such short acquaintance.

DORA. But we've known one another for *years*!

JEFF. But *Barnaby* doesn't know that!

DORA. He must! I just *told* him!

JEFF. I mean *before* that!

DORA. Before *what*?

JEFF. (*Totally lost, now, looks to* BARNABY *for help.*) Uh—care to give me a hand?

BARNABY. I wouldn't touch this conversation with a ten-foot pole.

DORA. Why? I don't follow you.

JEFF. You just answered your own question.

DORA. I beg—beg your— (*Has been fighting a sneeze on hesitations; now sneezes; then:*)—pardon?

JEFF. (*Instantly leads her up before fireplace, right of table,* BARNABY *moving up there left of table, during:*) Here, now, you're chilled to the bone! Silly little goose, crossing open fields at night in England!

BARNABY. Would some sherry help you?

DORA. Help me *what*?

JEFF. Warm *up*, darling.

DORA. (*Palms fireward.*) I'm *trying*, can't you see?

JEFF. Dora, I was finishing Barnaby's question, not giving an order!

DORA. Dearest, you can't *order* him to give you a sherry!

BARNABY. Look—why don't I just *get* it! (*Starts for sideboard.*) Before we die of thirst!

DORA. Oh, Wartsy, you're so thoughtful!

JEFF. (*As* BARNABY *halts short of sideboard and turns.*) *What* did you call him?

DORA. "Wartsy." It's a sort of pet name.

BARNABY. (*Slightly insulted.*) For a *toad*, perhaps!

DORA. (*Looks his way, prettily puzzled.*) But—surely you remember *why* I used to call you that, Barnaby?

BARNABY. (*Dubiously.*) Can't say as I do . . .

DORA. But how could you forget? You had the cutest little warts—three of them—on the back of your right ear. I used to fondle them while riding piggyback.

BARNABY. (*A hand going automatically to his ear.*) On the back of my—? Oh, *those*! I'd nearly forgotten.

DORA. But how could you? You said they used to get in the way whenever you combed your hair.

BARNABY. They did. That's why I had them removed. Beastly little things.

DORA. What? Removed? (*Starts toward him.*) Here, let me see!

BARNABY. (*Takes a backstep.*) Now, really, Dora—!

JEFF. Darling, stop pestering the poor man!

DORA. (*Stops, turns his way.*) But if he's had them taken off, whatever am I going to *call* him henceforth?

JEFF. "Barnaby" would be nice.

DORA. Oh, but my sweet, Barnaby always *was* nice!

Especially to me. No one else *ever* got to ride him piggy-back.

BARNABY. No one else *wanted* to!

DORA. I daresay that's true. And they would have looked silly, being adults. (*Abruptly sneezes again.*)

JEFF. Here, now, come back to fireside before you catch pneumonia!

BARNABY. (*Continues his interrupted move to sideboard as* JEFF *leads* DORA *to warm herself at the fire.*) And I'll just get us that sherry! (*He will pour three stem-goblets full of sherry, during:*)

DORA. (*Warming her hands again.*) Oh, but Jeff, however will I explain your presence to Great-Uncle Orion?

JEFF. There's no need. It's all explained. He believes me to be the short acquaintance of your cousin Cleo.

DORA. Nonsense, you're over six feet tall!

JEFF. The *acquaintance* is short, *I'm* not!

DORA. Well, you should *tell* Great-Uncle Orion at *once*! No point in confusing the old dear.

BARNABY. (*At sideboard, has just filled third glassful and restoppered the decanter when his glance falls upon the newspaper at the lower end of sideboard, and he picks it up, on:*) Here, now, what's this?

JEFF. What's what?

BARNABY. (*Takes a step or two toward him, indicating front page.*) Your picture, Mr. Barnett—right on the front page of the newspaper!

DORA. Really? How delightful! (*She and* JEFF *move to sideboard area to join him, each of them taking a glass of sherry, leaving* BARNABY'S *alone on sideboard, during:*)

JEFF. *My* picture, you say? I don't understand!

BARNABY. (*Reads from paper.*) "Mr. Jeffrey Barnett, a recent arrival to our shores, deplanes at the London airport. Mr. Barnett is a noted police reporter with the

*Dover, Delaware, Gazette,* but insisted to this reporter that he is here merely for pleasure, not business." (*While* BARNABY *is reading, and* JEFF *and* DORA *are peering at the paper from either side of him, a gloved hand emerges via the slot in the portrait over the sideboard, holding a small vial, and pours the contents into his sherry—turning it a poisonous shade of green—then withdraws; all this is done while he reads aloud, and hand is gone as he finishes:*) By heaven! This explains what Lady Barbara meant, earlier!

DORA. Great-Aunt Barbara? Meant about what?

BARNABY. (*Folds paper and replaces it on sideboard.*) She remarked that Jeff's pictures didn't do him justice. We all imagined she'd mistaken him for a motion-picture actor, or some such. But if she'd seen this edition of the newspaper—

JEFF. How could she? It's only just arrived a short while ago, and she had no opportunity to look at it.

BARNABY. Well, that's true enough, I daresay. And she did say "pictures," plural, and there's only the *one* in the paper . . .

DORA. Perhaps she meant the snapshots I sent her last month, in my regular biweekly letter.

JEFF. What, snapshots of me?

DORA. Of *us,* darling, on the night of our engagement party!

BARNABY. Oh, I say—congratulations are in order, then?

DORA. Well, hardly, Wartsy—mailing a letter is a minor achievement, at best.

BARNABY. (*Absently picking up his glass without looking at it.*) I meant the fact that you two plan to be married.

DORA. Jeff! That was supposed to be a secret!

JEFF. Darling, *I* didn't tell him!

DORA. Well, he *can't* be *psychic*!

BARNABY. Why *can't* I?

DORA. Well, *are* you?

BARNABY. Well, *no.*

DORA. (*To* JEFF.) There! So *how* did he know of our engagement?

JEFF. Darling, *you* told him!

DORA. Jeff, don't be stupid, if I *had* told him, I'd have certainly invited him to the *party,* but I hadn't, so I didn't, therefore he oughtn't.

BARNABY. Oughtn't *what*?

DORA. Know our *secret!*

BARNABY. *What* secret?

JEFF. That Dora and I are *engaged!*

DORA. There, you *did* tell him!

BARNABY. By George, she's right!

JEFF. But Dora, darling, he already *knew* when I just told him!

DORA. (*With insane logic.*) Now, *why* would you tell him something he already *knew*?

JEFF. (*Dizzily trying to reweave the fraying fabric of their chat.*) Because—that is—when he came downstairs—I mean—you said—or he said—or somebody said—

BARNABY. (*Sees he's floundering, interjects gallantly:*) Oh, what does it matter! The point is, I *do* know, now, and I should like to toast the soon-to-be bride! (*As he raises his glass,* JEFF *notices its color.*)

JEFF. Hold on—what's gone wrong with your sherry?

BARNABY. (*Looks at it, blinks, frowns, sets it on upstage end of table.*) It *does* look a bit odd, now that you mention it . . .

DORA. (*As* TRIO *stare down at it, curious, she points to a [totally imaginary] insect, tracking it with a forefinger during:*) Oh, look, there's a little fly on the rim of the glass! (TRIO *huddles in closer to watch the creature.*)

BARNABY. It's taking a sip—!

DORA. It's falling onto the table—!

JEFF. It's clutching its throat—!

DORA. It's rolling onto its back—!

BARNABY. (*Turns away squeamishly.*) I can't look!

DORA. (*Clutches* JEFF.) Oh, Jeffrey, my darling, hold me! (*Hides her face against his chest.*)

JEFF. (*The solo observer, now, watches a moment; then:*) All right. It's . . . all over!

(OTHERS *slowly turn back and solemnly look down at corpse.*)

DORA. Do you know—it reminds me of my late father.

BARNABY. Your father had six legs?

DORA. Certainly not!

BARNABY. Then I fail to see the resemblance.

DORA. I mean when he'd drink sherry—he'd take a sip, clutch his throat, roll onto his back—

JEFF. He died of drinking sherry?

DORA. Indirectly. He used to drink straight from the bottle, and one night he choked on the cork.

BARNABY. I say, I just noticed—*your* sherry is an entirely different color, Jeff—and *yours*, Dora . . .

DORA. They look alike to *me* . . . ?

BARNABY. Different from *mine*, not from each *other*! (*Puzzled, moves toward sideboard,* JEFF *and* DORA *following.*) Yet—how *can* it be? I poured all three from the same decanter . . . ?

JEFF. You don't suppose that—somebody or other—put something into it?

DORA. But when? How? We're the only three persons in the room!

BARNABY. And neither of you went anywhere *near* that decanter—and *I* certainly added nothing extraneous to my drink.

DORA. Of *course* you didn't, dear Barnaby. Why, you wouldn't hurt a *fly*!

JEFF. Yet that fly is most certainly *dead*!

BARNABY. Then how in the world did it *happen*?

JEFF. (*Thoughtfully, looking back toward poisoned sherry.*) I don't know. But I *do* think it might be wise to have your sherry analyzed!

DORA. But where would we get a psychiatrist?

JEFF. (*Impatiently.*) Dora, my love—

(*But he stops speaking as there comes a FLICKER OF LIGHTNING, in garden, followed immediately by a CLAP OF THUNDER, and ALL LIGHTS GO OUT for three seconds, and when LIGHTS COME UP, the glass of sherry has vanished from table [NOTE: This is done via a person in that cubbyhole, and henceforth anything or anyone that vanishes "Via Cubbyhole" will simply be indicated by the initials "VCH".]; TRIO reacts.*)

BARNABY. Look! The glass! It's gone!

DORA. How can we look at the glass if it's gone?

(TRIO *hurries to table, stares down at empty place.*)

JEFF. But—how *can* it be gone? No one was anywhere *near* it!

BARNABY. Never mind that! The important fact is—somebody tried to *poison* me, just now—and I can't for the life of me imagine *why*!

DORA. Perhaps it has something to do with the *tontine*!

JEFF. BARNABY. *What* tontine?

DORA. (*Prettily confused.*) There's more than *one*?

JEFF. Darling, *we* had no idea there was *any*, till this moment! At least, *I* didn't . . . ?

BARNABY. I assure you, neither did I! I mean, isn't that one of those things where a lot of people pool a lot of money, and survivor takes all? Well, *I'd* hardly be asked to join one—I'm practically *penniless!*

DORA. That's *true,* darling—Barnaby comes from a long line of famous paupers.

BARNABY. That's why I went off to America—to make my fortune.

JEFF. And—?

BARNABY. By the time I got there, all available fortunes had been made.

DORA. Oh, what a pity!

BARNABY. You can say *that* again!

DORA. Oh, what a pity!

JEFF. But darling—just who *are* the members of this tontine you mentioned?

DORA. Well, let me see—Great-Grandfather Farlow—he's hanging over the fireplace—(*Both* MEN *react, look, relax again, as she keeps speaking.*) set the thing up, shortly before I died and he went to America—or was it vice-versa? . . . Well, anyhow—the members include Great-Uncle Orion, Lady Barbara, Cleo Barton, Miss Barnsdale, and myself. Whoever outlives the others gets the *money*—and *I'm* the *youngest,* isn't that *keen!*

JEFF. Darling, I hate to dampen your enthusiasm, but has it occurred to you that a survivorship tontine might prove a temptation to a poisoner?

BARNABY. He's right, you know. If four of the five members perish, the last one would be sitting pretty.

JEFF. Sitting pretty in the electric chair, you mean. Suspicion would fall upon the sole survivor at once, after a string of four murders.

DORA. Oh, but darling, they don't use electric chairs in England. They merely hang people. It's ever so much cheaper.

JEFF. Darling, haven't I gotten through to you *yet*? You are in mortal danger!

DORA. Nonsense. If what you say is so, why in the world would the poisoner try to bump off *Barnaby*? *He's* not in the tontine.

BARNABY. Well, *that's* true enough . . .

JEFF. And yet—somebody *did* try to do you in, didn't' they! It doesn't make sense!

DORA. (*Smacks her palms together in delight.*) That's *it*!

JEFF/BARNABY. That's *what*?

DORA. Don't you see? If the *murder-attempt* didn't make any sense, then to find the *murderer,* all we have to do is look for a *person* who doesn't make sense! (JEFF *and* BARNABY *look at one another, then slowly return their gazes to* DORA, *unwilling to say what's on their minds.*) Jeff—? Barnaby—? Why are you looking at me that way?

JEFF. (*Dismisses the idea with a headshake.*) It's nothing, darling, nothing.

BARNABY. But let's get back to the point—why *would* anyone want to murder *me*? *I'm* the only one who stands to *gain* anything if the *others* die—but they gain *nothing* if *I* do!

JEFF. Hold on—what do you mean about gain? If you're not in the tontine—?

BARNABY. Well, obviously, old man, if all *five* persons died, that wouldn't matter—

DORA. It would certainly matter to *me*—being *one* of the five!

BARNABY. I mean matter money-wise. With all five gone, the money would revert to the estate, and *I* would be the sole surviving *relative,* and— (*Stops, frowns.*) Do you know—that's set me thinking—I wonder if—oh, it's an absolutely *ridiculous* suspicion, but—it would certainly explain the poison in my sherry just now—

JEFF. *What* would, Barnaby? What have you just thought of?

BARNABY. I thought—no, wait—I mustn't betray a confidence! Not until I've asked about—

JEFF. But your confidante could be a killer!

DORA. Barnaby, can't you tell us without naming names?

BARNABY. Hmmm. *That* might be all right, I daresay. Then if my suspicion should prove true, I could name the name!

JEFF. Barnaby, there's a killer on the loose! Stop trying to ease your conscience and tell us what you know!

BARNABY. Well—for starters—two of the people at this party are imposters!

DORA. Three, if you count Jeff. (*To* JEFF.) Short acquaintance of Cleo, indeed! (*To* BARNABY.) Or *were* you counting Jeff?

BARNABY. No-no, not at all. But you're right, of course. That *does* make three.

JEFF. Barnaby, will you get *on* with it! Who *are* the imposters?

BARNABY. I can't tell you. That's the confidence I spoke of. Gave my word, old man!

JEFF. If *you* ever hope to be an old man, *forget* what you told your confidante, and *tell* us!

DORA. But darling, shouldn't he tell us *before* he forgets?

JEFF. That's *not* what I meant!

DORA. But that's what you *said*!

JEFF. (*Grasps her upper arms, speaks gently but firmly.*) Dora, my dearest darling—shut up! (*Turns to* BARNABY, *but continues to hold* DORA.) Now, before it's too late, will you *please* tell us—

BARNABY. Oh . . . very well! (*Moves to position upstage of table, leans fists on table edge, stares determinedly out front, then speaks.*) The names of the two imposters *are*—

(*Almost simultaneously, we have LIGHTNING/THUN-
DERCLAP/BLACKOUT; BLACKOUT lasts only
a few seconds; when LIGHTS COME UP, of
course,* BARNABY *has vanished* [VCH].)

JEFF. (*Releases* DORA, *aghast.*) Look! Barnaby! He's
gone!
DORA. How can I look at Barnaby if he's gone?
JEFF. (*Rushes to spot, looks left, right, under table,
into hearth.*) This is impossible! Mind-boggling! He was
standing right here!
DORA. Perhaps he stepped out for some fresh air?
JEFF. *Stepped* out? Dora, in the short time the lights
were out, he couldn't have made it through those garden
doors if he'd been shot from a *cannon*!
DORA. Well, he must have gone *someplace,* because
he's *definitely* not *here*!
JEFF. (*Moves back to her at sideboard.*) But Dora,
don't you see that his disappearance is impossible?!

(*At this moment, another LIGHTNING/THUNDER-
CLAP/BLACKOUT occurs, and when LIGHTS
COME UP, we see* BARNABY *standing where he was,
at upstage end of table, a startled look on his face.*)

DORA. Barnaby! You're back! (*Then he topples face-
first across table, and we see the hilt of a dagger jutting
from between his shoulderblades.*) Barnaby! (*Points at
dagger.*) Your back! (*She and* JEFF *rush to flank him,*
JEFF *right,* DORA *left, so that they are near downstage
area of table sides, near his head; as they arrive,* BAR-
NABY *raises his face to our view.*)
BARNABY. P-p-*paper*—!
DORA. Oh, yes, of course! (*Rushes to sideboard, gets
newspaper, rushes back saying:*) What section, sports or
the funnies?

BARNABY. Wr-wr-*writing* paper!

JEFF. Oh, of course! (*Rushes to desk, yanks drawer open, grabs out stationery, rushes back saying:*) It's monogrammed . . . is that all right?

DORA. Isn't there any plain?

JEFF. I could check the other drawers—

(BARNABY *makes an incoherent noise of frustration.*)

DORA. He's trying to *tell* us something! (*In her eagerness to lean her ear close to his face, she leans her hand on dagger-handle, and* BARNABY *yelps in mingled pain and rage; she reacts instantly, pulls hand away.*) Oh! Sorry!

JEFF. Here's that paper you wanted! (*Sets it on lower edge of table, and* BARNABY *wearily lets his face drop on-to it.*)

DORA. Wouldn't a pillow be more comfortable?

BARNABY. (*Raises face.*) P-p-*pen*!

JEFF. (*Pats his pockets frantically, stops.*) I don't have one!

DORA. Would a pencil do?

BARNABY. (*A weary gasp.*) Yes—!

DORA. I haven't got one!

JEFF. The desk! There must be a pen or pencil at the desk!

(*He and* DORA *rush there, rummaging through the drawers, and over their business and dialogue, we can see* BARNABY *laboriously scribbling something slowly on the paper below his face with the tip of his forefinger.*)

DORA. Here's a bottle of ink!

JEFF. A stapler!

DORA. A ruler!

JEFF. A box of rubberbands!

DORA. An eraser!

JEFF. A paperweight!

DORA. (*Holds it aloft triumphantly.*) A pencil!

JEFF. Quick, give it to me!

DORA. Why? *I* found it!

JEFF. (*Takes hold of pencil, which she continues to grasp.*) What does that matter!

DORA. Fair is fair!

JEFF. Dora, will you *please*—

(*The pencil snaps in half; BOTH stare at the part they hold, then abruptly race back to BARNABY, who is weakly waving a piece of paper at them by now.*)

DORA. Oh, look, Jeff—he's fingerwritten something in the dust on the paper!

JEFF. (*They are now flanking BARNABY again.*) What? Let me see that! (*Grabs paper, reads:*) Bar! The killer's in the bar! (*Drops paper to floor as he and DORA rush to sideboard.*)

DORA. There's no one here!

(*Behind them, BARNABY is making weary headshakes, his lips silently forming a string of "no-no-no" syllabications.*)

JEFF. Perhaps we misunderstood! Quick, back to Barnaby!

(*They race back and flank him again, as before.*)

DORA. Barnaby, what is the *meaning* of what you wrote? (*On stressed word, absently pounds fist on dagger-handle.*)

BARNABY. (*Beyond pain, now, but well into frustrated fury.*) Will you *stop* that—?!

DORA. Oh! Sorry!

JEFF. But the word you wrote—what does it mean?

BARNABY. (*Weakly.*) Name . . . name of killer . . . too weak to finish it . . .

DORA. Ah! So it must be Rosalind *Bar*stow! I never *did* trust her!

JEFF. Wait! It could just as well be Cleo *Bar*ton!

(*Throughout their conjectures, of course,* BARNABY *is trying vainly to get a word in, but they pay him no mind.*)

JEFF. Or your old governess Miss *Bar*nsdale!

DORA. Oh, dear, I *do* hope it's not Great-Aunt *Bar*bara! There's *twice* as much evidence against *her!*

JEFF. Evidence? *What* evidence?

DORA. Well, "Barbara" has "bar" in it *twice!*

JEFF. At least we know it's not Medkins or Magnolia!

DORA. *Who* are Medkins and Magnolia?

JEFF. Oh, that's right, you don't know them. Butler and maid your Uncle Orion hired for the party.

DORA. Ah! I almost forgot him! It can't be my uncle either!

JEFF. Well, hold on—after all, he *is* a baronet—*that* begins with "B-A-R" too!

DORA. (*Takes an abrupt backstep.*) How dare you! Why, he's one of the kindliest, nicest—you should be ashamed of yourself, Jeff Barnett! . . . Oh! *Your* name has a "B-A-R"!

JEFF. Darling, *I* didn't do it! I was right there with you!

DORA. *Till* the lights went out! *Then* what happened!

JEFF. They came right *on* again! And I was *still* over there with you!

DORA. (*Half-convinced.*) Welllll . . . (*Then, suddenly.*) I say! As long as Barnaby's not *dead* yet—why don't we just *ask* him!

JEFF. (*Angry at himself, slaps palm down on dagger-handle on:*) Of *course*! (BARNABY *gives final cry, flops face down, and dies.*) Oopsy! Ha-ha! Well, he would have died soon enough, anyway!

DORA. Of course he would, dearest!

(*Then* BOTH *look up—and left and right, as events occur—as first* ORION *and* ROSALIND *step into room from garden, and stop, then* MEDKINS *and* MAGNOLIA *step in from kitchen, and stop,* BARNSY *enters from cellar, and stops,* BARBARA *descends a few stairs down staircase into view, and stops, and* CLEO *steps in from front hall, and stops; each entrance, however, occurs on a speech, and the speeches are:*)

ORION. Here now!

ROSALIND. What's this?

MEDKINS. It's Mr. Folcey!

MAGNOLIA. He's been stabbed!

BARNSY. Is he dead?

BARBARA. Why, look, everyone, it's dear little Dora!

CLEO. (*Final entrant.*) Oh, no! *No*! NO! *NO*!

BARBARA. Well, it *looks* like Dora—?

JEFF. Hold on! Everybody stay right where you are! There's been a murder! Tell me where each of you has been during the past five minutes!

BARBARA. I beg your pardon?

DORA. (*Grabs up paper, uses tip-half of pencil, during:*) Here, Jeff, you check out the others, while I write down the question for her!

JEFF. (*As* DORA *scribbles.*) Now please tell me—it's very important—

ORION. Well, Rosalind and I went for a stroll in the garden after dinner.

MEDKINS. And Magnolia and I were cleaning up the dishes left from dinner.

BARNSY. And I was in the wine-cellar trying to find an after-dinner liqueur.

CLEO. (*As* DORA *takes note to* BARBARA, *who reads it carefully.*) And I stayed in the dining room dawdling over my dinner.

BARBARA. (*Hands note back to* DORA, *announces:*) And I always take a nap after dinner.

JEFF. (*Frowns.*) Well, Dora—what does it all *mean*?

DORA. (*Despondently.*) We've missed *dinner*!

(*And as* ALL *stare uneasily at one another—*)

## THE CURTAIN FALLS

## ACT TWO

*Curtain rises on the parlor of Marlgate, much later that
same night. Used glasses,* DORA'S *coat and baggage, the tray of* hors d'oeuvre *and* BARNABY *have
been cleared. The garden doors are closed.*

*At curtain-rise, we find all surviving persons onstage,
thusly:* BARNSY *is seated on desk chair, which is now
turned to face toward stage left, that is, into the
room;* ORION *is seated on parson's bench;* MAGNOLIA
*stands just inside kitchen-exit archway;* CLEO *is
seated at upper end of right settee,* ROSALIND *at
lower end;* BARBARA *is seated at upper end of left
settee,* DORA *at lower end;* MEDKINS *is standing
before sideboard;* JEFF *stands before fireplace, facing table. [There will be a recurrent "reaction" of
various parties in this act, which goes thusly: The
person hunches up the shoulders slightly, clenches
both fists before the stomach, juts out lower lip,
narrows the eyelids, and lets the eyes go shiftily
from left-to-right-to-left-to-right for a moment;
this movement is to symbolize "deep-seated guilt";
for practical purposes, the stage-direction given for
this hunch/clench/etc. reaction will be simply given
as "HC."] At rise of curtain,* ALL *are warily watch-
ing* JEFF, *whom we meet in mid-speech:*

JEFF. Now, I don't intend to give offense to anyone
present, but there *has* been a ghastly murder committed
here, tonight, and before the police arrive, I think it is in
the best interests of *all* of us that we do what we can to

43

find out which one of us is the *killer*. Do you agree? (ALL *move uneasily, flicking glances at one another.*) Well? *Do* you? *I'd* certainly feel a *lot* safer if I knew which one of you to *avoid*!

CLEO. And so would I!

ROSALIND. Yes, let's find out who killed Barnaby, by all means!

BARBARA. What *I'd* like to know is, *who* murdered *Barnaby*!

BARNSY. (*Squints toward sound.*) Who said that?

ORION. Damn and blast! Between your eyes and Barbara's ears, we'll never get *anything* cleared up!

DORA. Then we may as well go to bed!

MAGNOLIA. With a murderer on the prowl?!

MEDKINS. Magnolia, *all* the bedrooms have stout locks on the doors.

MAGNOLIA. What if he's in the room *with* you when you *lock* it?!

ORION. And who says the murderer is a *he*? It might be a woman, you know!

BARNSY. Nonsense. Barnaby was stabbed. A lady always uses poison—it's much more polite.

DORA. But the *first* attempt on Barnaby's life *was* a glass of poison!

ROSALIND. That might mean there are *two* murderers in our midst! A poisoner *and* a stabber!

MAGNOLIA. I wish you wouldn't *say* things like that!

ORION. Be calm, Magnolia. Rosalind is mistaken. The most we could have in our midst is one *actual* murderer and one *would-be* murderer, do you see? The *dagger* worked, but the poison *didn't*.

MAGNOLIA. If you think you've soothed my nerves, you're even dumber than you look!

BARNSY. Magnolia! That's *no* way to speak about one's employer!

MAGNOLIA. If you could *see* him, you'd *agree* with me!

JEFF. May I *please* have some quiet?! This bickering is getting us nowhere!

MEDKINS. Mr. Barnett is quite right. The time could be much better spent by learning which of you people committed the murder.

CLEO. Why are you excluding yourself?

MEDKINS. Why, by the name the late Mr. Folcey was attempting to write down when he died. It could be anybody but myself, Magnolia and Miss Dunstock.

DORA. Oh! That's right! What a relief! I'd feel just *terrible* if Jeff felt he had to avoid *me*!

JEFF. Hold on—I've done a bit of questioning since the murder, and I find that suspicion is much wider than we'd at first imagined—!

DORA. But—how *can* it be? Dear old Wartsy quite definitely wrote "B-A-R" before he died, so the killer could only be someone like Miss Barstow—

ROSALIND. (*Instantly, defensively.*) Or Miss Barton—!

CLEO. And what about Barnsy?!

BARNSY. Don't forget Orion is a baronet!

ORION. And don't forget Barbara has *two* strikes against her!

(ALL *have shifted to hear each speaker—in* BARBARA'S *case, of course, she merely* tries *to hear—and now,* ALL *turn toward* BARBARA *in expectation of her rebuttal, on:*)

DORA. Aunt Barbara, darling, it's *your* turn!

BARBARA. Shouldn't we all be trying to find out who killed Barnaby?

ORION. It's no use, Dora. She'll *never* find out what's going on! But, in our catalogue of suspects, let us not forget Mr. Barnett, himself!

CLEO. Who *tricked* me into bringing him up here to the house!

ROSALIND. Who concealed his engagement to Dora!

BARNSY. And who was alone with Barnaby when he died!

ORION. Oh, but *Dora* was with him, Barnsy.

MAGNOLIA. That's as *good* as being alone!

MEDKINS. *Really*, Magnolia, mind your manners! (*Then, to* JEFF.) But, sir, what did you mean, a moment ago, when you said that neither Magnolia nor I was above suspicion—there is no "B-A-R" in either of our names, so I fail to see—

JEFF. Ah, but *you* were the person "tending *bar*," as it were, for the party, and *could* somehow have introduced poison into that glass! (MEDKINS *does HC.*)

MAGNOLIA. Well, *I* never *touched* anything *near* that sideboard—bottle *or* glass!

JEFF. But a quick phone-call to the agency that assigned you to this house led to the interesting information that you are only working as a maid to earn enough money to finish attending *law* school—in other words, you hope to become a member of the *bar*! (MAGNOLIA *does HC.*)

ORION. Aha! And we only have their word for it that, at the time of the murder, they were washing up the dinner dishes! If they are both under suspicion—a man and woman, who could be the stabber and poisoner quite easily—naturally their alibis could be faked!

JEFF. Ah, but so could *all* your alibis, I'm afraid, Mr. Leduc. For instance, you say that you and Miss Barstow were out for a stroll after dinner—but really, now—in the middle of a *thunderstorm*? (ORION *and* ROSALIND *do HCs.*) And Miss Barnsdale says she was in the wine-cellar seeking an after-dinner drink, when we all *know* she couldn't possibly read the labels on any of the bottles! (BARNSY *does HC.*) Now, Cleo claims she dawdled over dinner, but from what I gather from the rest of you, she couldn't *abide* the boiled mutton, and left the table *early*, saying she was going to her room for a smoke! (CLEO *does HC.*)

DORA. But what of Aunt Barbara? She always *does* take a nap after dinner—?!

ROSALIND. No, wait! Just as we were going in to dinner, she told me that she had already *had* her nap!

JEFF. So you see—there is *no one* in this room who is above suspicion!

DORA. Oh, Jeff!

JEFF. I didn't mean *you*, dearest!

CLEO. (*Stands.*) And why the hell *not*?! After all, the only account we have of the murder is what the *two* of *you* said—how do we know you didn't pair up to bump him off and then make the whole story up to mislead us?!

DORA. (*Stands.*) Because I'm your own flesh and blood, and Jeff has an honest face!

BARNSY. (*Stands, moves toward* JEFF *at fireplace.*) He *has*? Let me have a look at it!

MAGNOLIA. (*Moves downstage so that she follows* BARNSY *toward* JEFF.) What's his *looks* got to do with anything?!

ROSALIND. (*Comes to her feet.*) Yes, *what*?! We merely suspect him of *murder*, we *never* said he was *dishonest*!

BARBARA. (*As* MEDKINS *moves toward fireside group.*) Why is everybody standing up? (*As* OTHERS *all look toward her, parson's bench rotates into wall, carrying a startled* ORION *with it, and Side #2 of bench settles into place.*)

MEDKINS. Will somebody *please* tell Lady Barbara what's going on?!

DORA. Who's got a pencil and paper?

ROSALIND. Ye gods, are we going to *sit* here all night while you write everything *down* for the old dodo?! (*Turns toward spot she last saw* ORION.) Orion, I appeal to you—! . . . Orion? (OTHERS *now look toward bench.*) Where in the world did he go?

MAGNOLIA. I'll bet *he's* the killer, and he's made a *run* for it!

CLEO. Oh, *come* now, Magnolia, the old foof could barely *walk*!

(ALL *have moved into area of bench, now, peering about.*)

BARBARA. Excuse me, but what are we all looking for?

BARNSY. Orion, dear. (*Squints toward bench.*) Does anybody see him?

MEDKINS. He may have gone into the garden.

CLEO. No, the doors are still shut. We'd have heard them open.

ROSALIND. The kitchen, perhaps?

MAGNOLIA. He'd have had to move awfully fast—and we'd have seen him.

JEFF. But he didn't cross the room—I'd swear to that!

DORA. Well, people don't simply *vanish*, darling!

JEFF. You're forgetting what happened earlier, before Barnaby was stabbed!

CLEO. *What* happened?

DORA. He vanished. He was standing right there, by the table, and all at once the lights went out, and when they came on he was gone!

ROSALIND. Why haven't you told us this before?

JEFF. It seemed a rather minor occurrence, in the light of what happened afterward.

BARNSY. Yes, a disappearance is nothing compared to a murder.

DORA. So it simply slipped my mind.

MAGNOLIA. *What* mind?!

MEDKINS. *Really*, Magnolia!

MAGNOLIA. Why should I be respectful? I was hired for a party, and the party's over!

ROSALIND. But Jeff—Dora—tell us more about this vanishment just before *Barnaby* was *killed*.

BARBARA. Oh, he certainly was! *Extremely* skilled! He was one of the best ever!

DORA. Aunt Barbara, what are you saying?

BARNSY. That Barnaby was *skilled*. She misunderstood Orion's fiancee.

CLEO. What?! Rosalind—do you mean—you and Orion—?!

MAGNOLIA. Talk about your May-December marriages!

ROSALIND. Magnolia, I would hardly call Orion of December age!

MAGNOLIA. I *didn't* mean *him*!

ROSALIND. How dare you!

MEDKINS. There, now, you wicked girl, see what you've done! (*Starts towing her kitchenward.*) Speaking before you're spoken to, insulting the guests, and showing no respect for anyone at all, just because there's a *killer* on the loose—! (*They are gone.*)

ROSALIND. The *rudest* girl . . . !

CLEO. Never mind her! *I* want to find out when you got engaged to Orion!

ROSALIND. Well, *I'd* rather find out what Barbara seems to think Barnaby was skilled at doing!

JEFF. And *I'd* like to find out which one of us is a cold-blooded *killer*!

BARBARA. Has anybody seen Orion? He was sitting right over there . . .

BARNSY. Will somebody *please* give Lady Barbara a *scorecard* before I *scream*?!

BARBARA. Ice cream? That sounds delightful! Who's *got* some?!

BARNSY. (*True to her word.*) Aaaaaaaah!

CLEO. Don't *do* that, Barnsy!

ROSALIND. Oh, never *mind* the old muttonhead! (BARNSY *reacts.*) What's become of *Orion*?!

DORA. Perhaps his disappearance has something to do with the tontine!

JEFF. Of course! That *must* be it!

BARNSY. (*To* ROSALIND.) Who are you calling a muttonhead?!

ROSALIND. Barbara, of course!

BARNSY. (*Mollified.*) Oh, well, *that's* all right!

CLEO. Will *you* two stop bickering before *I* scream?!

BARBARA. Yes, but who's *got* some?!

CLEO. Aaaaaaaah!

JEFF. *All* of you stop it! There's a *killer* in our midst, and we've got to figure out the *motive* for murder before anyone *else* gets dispatched!

ROSALIND. Jeff's right! Let's put our *brains* together!

CLEO. Why leave *Dora* out?

BARNSY. Now, *stop* that, Cleo! Dora isn't a dunce! She's just—broadcasting on an unfamiliar frequency.

DORA. Why, *thank* you, Barnsy . . . I *think*.

CLEO. The *hell* you do!

JEFF. Ladies, ladies! There's a *murder* to be solved, remember?!

BARNSY. Yes-yes, of course! Come now, let's all sit down and pool whatever information we possess!

(*Over next few lines,* CLEO *will sit at downstage end of right settee with* ROSALIND *on her left,* DORA *at downstage end of left settee with* BARBARA *on her right,* JEFF *will take a stance between bench and right settee, and* BARNSY *will stand before fireplace facing table.*)

JEFF. Now, let's get matters straight! First off—Barnaby was murdered, and probably by someone in this house.

CLEO. But why couldn't it be an outsider—a roving lunatic, or somesuch?

BARNSY. Impossible! It's pouring rain outside—there'd have been all sorts of mud and wet footprints on the floor. Do you agree, Jeffrey?

JEFF. Absolutely! *And* our killer had to know something of the layout of this house.

ROSALIND. Why do you say that?

JEFF. Because of the subtle way the poison was introduced into Barnaby's glass, and the way he disappeared and reappeared—who knows?, there may be secret panels and such in this old house—how would an outsider know about them?

DORA. Then it's settled. We can rule the outsider out.

CLEO. Now, wait—what's to prevent a stray madman from creeping into the house, *accidentally* discovering the panels, or whatever, and—

BARNSY. And what? Madmen aren't selective in their murders. Yet it seems that Barnaby was singled out for killing.

ROSALIND. Otherwise the killer would have put poison in *all three* glasses, is that what you mean, Barnsy?

BARNSY. Exactly. But he didn't, so we know Barnaby was the sole intended victim.

DORA. Perhaps the madman just didn't have enough poison to go around.

JEFF. But he *did* have a *dagger*, dear. He could have used *that* more than the one time, do you see?

CLEO. Then it comes right back to *Barnaby*. It *always* comes back to *him*.

ROSALIND. So, if we can deduce why *he* was murdered—

DORA. But we can't. That's the bewildering part of the whole thing. He had no money—he wasn't a member of the tontine—and it certainly can't be something he *knew* about any of us, because he hadn't been in touch with any of us for years and years.

JEFF. Now, wait, Dora—he *did* know *something*, remember! He said that two of the people in this house were imposters!

BARNSY. He *what*?!

ROSALIND. You didn't mention that before!

CLEO. Which two people did he say?

DORA. That's the whole problem—he was just *about* to tell us, when—when it happened— the *murder.*

BARNSY. Odd. Decidedly odd. It's all so topsy-turvy.

JEFF. What do you mean?

BARNSY. I mean the motive—it's all backwards. You see, as the poor relation of our family, Barnaby had a *marvelous* motive for killing all of *us*—but none of us has the *slightest* reason for wanting *him* dead.

CLEO. (*Jumps to her feet.*) But we *must* have!

DORA. *I* certainly don't!

ROSALIND. (*Stands.*) *I* know what Cleo means. Barnaby's murder is a *fact*—and a murder must have a *motive*—and we're the only people who could have *done* it—so—?

BARNSY. (*Nods.*) So there *is* a motive—a motive we haven't *thought* of, yet—but a motive nonetheless.

JEFF. (*Moving toward point above right settee, beside* BARNSY.) And one of us knows that motive. We're all *showing* total ignorance, *honest* ignorance in most cases, but *one* of us is only *play*-acting!

BARBARA. He *was* very good at it, you know.

DORA. Good at what, Aunt Barbara? Who?

BARNSY. Oh, pay her no mind. Orion told me during dinner that she's gotten some fool notion that she and Barnaby used to—used to—(*Frowns, considering.*)

JEFF. What is it, Barnsy?

BARNSY. (*Icily.*) "*Miss* Barnsdale," if you don't mind. Pet-names on such very short acquaintance are quite rude, young man!

CLEO. Oh, Barnsy, come off it! We're seeking a killer! To hell with protocol!

ROSALIND. Cleo's right, Barnsy—tell us, quickly, what have you thought of?!

BARNSY. (*Still a bit ruffled, composes herself a bit, and:*) Well, the fascinating notion has just popped into my head that-(*There is that LIGHTNING/THUNDER/ BLACKOUT, and in the darkness we can hear her continuing:*) No! Stop! Let me go! Aaaaaaaah! (*LIGHTS COME UP, and she has vanished [VCH]; JEFF is now standing directly upstage of table where she had been; DORA and BARBARA now come to their feet like the others.*)

DORA. Jeff! What in the world have you done with Barnsy?!

JEFF. (*Baffled, wide-eyed.*) What? Why—nothing! She was right here—and now—?!

(*Bench revolves back to Side #1, and we see ORION, bound and gagged, sitting there, pop-eyed and irate, but OTHERS onstage do not yet realize he has returned, during:*)

CLEO. (*Tries to move past JEFF.*)This place is a death-trap! I'm going up to my room!

JEFF. (*Stops her.*) Alone?!

CLEO. (*Abruptly snuggles against him.*) Why, *Jeff*, how very *friendly* of you!

DORA. Oh, Jeff, how *could* you!

JEFF. (*Prying free of CLEO's grasp.*) I *meant* she could be in *danger* upstairs!

CLEO. (*Cuddles close again.*) Why, *Jeff*, how very *macho* of you!

DORA. I thought *I* was the woman you loved!

JEFF. (*Prying free again.*) *I'm* talking about *murder*!

DORA. (*Angrily.*) And I'm *thinking* about murder!

ROSALIND. (*Has turned to move up toward* JEFF *and* CLEO, *sees* ORION.) *Look*! He's *back*!

(ROSALIND *and* OTHERS *all rush to* ORION, *during:*)

CLEO. Who tied him up?

DORA. Who gagged him?

JEFF. Thank heaven he's alive!

BARBARA. Orion, this is no time to play cowboys and Indians!

(*They will get him untied, during:*)

CLEO. How did he get *back* here with his feet tied?

DORA. He must have *hopped*!

ROSALIND. But why didn't we *hear* him?

JEFF. Look, let's get his *mouth* free, and maybe he can *tell* us! (*He undoes knot of gag at back of* ORION'S *head, and* ORION *gratefully yanks it away from his mouth.*)

ORION. Sherry! I need a glass of sherry!

BARBARA. Water! Somebody get the poor man a glass of water!

ORION. I said *sherry*!

ROSALIND. Oh, darling, I was so terrified when you vanished!

(*Over next eight speeches,* ORION *will do his determined-but-slow-progress "geisha-shuffle" directly across to sideboard,* OTHERS *following him, with* CLEO *last in line, so that she will be at the cubbyhole point at the proper moment.*)

ORION. Damn and blast! I'll get the sherry *myself*!

BARBARA. Someone get him a glass of water!

ROSALIND. Oh, shut up, Lady Barbara!

DORA. You'll have to insult her *much* louder than that, Rosalind.

JEFF. Will you all be *quiet* so Orion can tell us where he's *been*?!

CLEO. Yes, Orion, just where *have* you been?!

ROSALIND. Yes, one moment you were there, the next you had gone! Where *were* you?

BARBARA. After he has his water, let's ask him where he's been!

(ORION *is at sideboard, now, pouring himself a sherry, with—in order—*ROSALIND, JEFF, DORA, BARBARA *and* CLEO *in a line behind him, all facing in his direction.*)

ORION. (*Turns, with glass of sherry in his hand.*) Well, it's been the most extraordinary experience—I was seated over there, on the bench, when all at once—(*Notices, frowns.*) I say—what's become of Barnsy?

JEFF. We were hoping *you* might tell *us*!

DORA. You see, Uncle Orion, she seems to have vanished.

ORION. Vanished? Barnsy?

CLEO. Yes, she was standing right in this very spot—(*Realizes her own potential peril.*) Oh, dear! (*And we have the LIGHTNING/THUNDER/BLACKOUT [let's start calling it "LTB" from here on].*) No! Stop! Help!

(*LIGHTS COME UP and* CLEO *is gone; all but* ORION *rush back to where she last stood [she's gone VCH, of course], during:*)

ROSALIND. Oh, this is terrible! First Barnaby—!

DORA. Then Uncle Orion—!

JEFF. Then Barnsy—!

ROSALIND. And now, dear sweet Cleo!

DORA. I thought you *hated* her—?

ROSALIND. I *did*, but I'd hardly admit that *now*! It would give me a motive.

ORION. (*During their tableward rush, has drained his sherry, and is now pouring himself another one, shaking his head sadly.*) This is my fault! All of it! If I hadn't been so greedy—!

JEFF. *What*?! Then you *do* know something! (*Is moving toward him, now,* DORA *and* ROSALIND *following.*) *Tell* us, quickly, before something *else* happens!

ORION. (*Sets untasted sherry on sideboard for a moment.*) Well, you see, the reason I asked the family to return home to Marlgate for this gathering was—

(*LTB; ad-libbed cries of dismay from* ALL *onstage; then LIGHTS come up and* BARNSY *is standing where we last saw her, blinking and looking bewildered.*)

DORA. Barnsy! You're back!

JEFF. (*As he and* WOMEN *rush to* BARNSY, *with* ORION *shuffling after.*) Don't *say* that, darling! Remember what happened when you said it to Barnaby!

ROSALIND. Barnsy! Where have you been?!

BARNSY. Well, really, it's the most extraordinary thing, but— Oh! It's gone! (*Is fumbling briefly inside the bosom of her dress.*) I had it on a nice, strong chain—but it's gone!

ORION. (*Stops his shuffle, frantically feels at his pockets.*) Good heavens! So is mine! I had it right in my pocket!

BARBARA. I say, isn't that Barnsy? But what's become of Cleo?

JEFF. Hold it, all of you! What's gone? What are you all talking about?

ORION. Why, the pigeon-thingy, of course!

BARNSY. "*Jambule*," Orion, "*Jambule*"! (*This is pronounced "zhom-BOOL".*)

ORION. Oh, hang your fancy French words, Barnsy! It's a pigeon-thingy, and it's gone!

ROSALIND. Orion—Barnsy—what *are* you two babbling about?!

DORA. Well, you see, Great-Grandfather Farlow used to keep carrier pigeons.

JEFF. (*When she volunteers no further elucidation.*) *And*—?!

DORA. Well, isn't it *obvious*?

JEFF. (*Ready to sob.*) Isn't *what* obvious?!

DORA. Well, the messages had to go into *something*, darling. A pigeon doesn't have any pockets.

ROSALIND. Wait—are you talking about one of those tiny little *whatsies* that fasten onto the creature's *leg*?

BARNSY. It is called a "*jambule*," Rosalind.

DORA. *Or* a pigeon-thingy.

BARNSY. Dora, that term is slangy, ridiculous and totally inappropriate!

DORA. But it sounds so cute!

JEFF. (*At wit's end.*) *Please*! (OTHERS *jump, startled.*) Let's not bicker about proper wording! Let's hear why these *gizmos* are so damned *important*!

DORA. Why, they each hold a part of the *limerick*, darling.

JEFF. *What* limerick?!

ORION. Why, the one that Father made up before he died, of course.

ROSALIND. "Father"?

DORA. Uncle Orion's *father* was *my* great-*grand*father, Rosalind. His name was "Farlow," and he was *ever* so nice. *That's* why Uncle had him painted and hung!

JEFF. Never *mind* that! *I* want to know the *significance* of the *gizmos*!

BARNSY. *Jambules*!

ROSALIND. Whatsies!

ORION. Pigeon-thingies!

BARBARA. Why, Barnsy, what's become of your nice chain with the little leg-luggage on it?

JEFF. Oh, *shut up*, all of you! Not another word! Don't say one more thing! (ALL *stand there, staring at him, slightly hurt.*) That's better. Now—explain about that limerick you mentioned. (ALL *stand there, staring at him, slightly hurt.*) Damn it all, I didn't mean you had to be silent *forever*!

(*Next five speeches are all said at the same time:*)

ORION. Well, just before Father cashed in his chips—

DORA. When Great-Grandfather was on his deathbed—

BARNSY. He had all these roles of message-paper—

BARBARA. Why is everybody acting so nervous—?

ROSALIND. I don't have the slightest idea what's going on—!

(JEFF *sags disconsolately, covering his face with his hands; as* OTHERS *focus apologetically on him, that gloved hand once more enters via portrait and green-poisons* ORION'S *sherry, then pops back out of view again.*)

DORA. Darling, whatever is the matter?

JEFF. (*Uncovers face, stares at her in unbelief; then:*) I'll *tell* you what's the matter! There has been a brutal murder, several strange disappearances, and now, apparent thefts of some sort of message-containers of *vast* significance, and we may all be in hideous peril from the still-unknown *killer*, and all you people can do is stand around and *babble* at me!

ORION. *Babble*?!

BARNSY. *What* babble?!

DORA. It all makes perfect sense to *me* . . . ?!

JEFF. All right, then—*you* explain it!

DORA. Which part?

JEFF. (*In despair.*) Oh, damn!

ROSALIND. Listen, all of you—*I'm* just as befuddled as *Jeff*, and I've known you all a *lot* longer. Can't we take this thing in easy stages?

BARBARA. Oh, there's nothing easy about being on the stage, my dear. Why, I remember Mrs. Michaels always telling the class—

BARNSY. (*Interjects.*) Barbara, please—!

BARBARA. (*Hasn't heard or, nor paused in her speech.*)—how very *difficult* it was to play a role—like that Mr. Tate, or Lawson—the one from Connover Station—

JEFF. *Who*?

ORION. She means *Barnaby*, old chap. Never *did* get his name right. But then, she hardly ever gets *anything* right!

BARNSY. She imagines the two of them used to be on the *stage* together.

DORA. Aunt Barbara and Barnaby? But how silly!

ROSALIND. *Please*! We're getting off the track *entirely*! What was all that blather about a *limerick*, or something?

ORION. Why, that was the clue to where Father has hidden the *gold*, do you see?

JEFF. Ah! Now we're *getting* somewhere! (*Then, blankly:*) *What* gold?!

DORA. Why, *our* gold, of course. You see, darling, Uncle Orion, Aunt Barbara, Cleo, Barnsy, and myself all converted whatever cash we had into gold, for that *tontine*. Then Great-Grandfather took it and *hid it*—

ROSALIND. Well, *that* was a lousy trick!

BARNSY. But you don't *understand*—we all *asked* him to hide it.

JEFF. Hide your gold? What in the world *for*?

DORA. So we wouldn't know where it *was*, of course.

JEFF. (*To* ROSALIND.) Maybe *I'm* the crazy one!

ROSALIND. No, you're not, it sounds *just* as stupid to me!

ORION. But what could be simpler? You see, when we first *bought* the gold, it was a mere thirty-five dollars an ounce. Nowadays, of course, it's worth a small fortune.

BARNSY. A *large* fortune, Orion. Gold is currently worth twenty times as much.

DORA. But Great-Grandfather Farlow didn't want any of us succumbing to temptation, so—

JEFF. Temptation to *what*?

ORION. To cash in our portion *early*, don't you see?

BARNSY. He *suspected* the price of gold would rise, and didn't want us to cash it in before it reached its utmost limit.

DORA. But if we'd *found* it, of course, then we *would* have before it *did*, and it wouldn't have the *chance* to!

ROSALIND. My *mind* must be going—I'm beginning to understand *Dora*!

JEFF. But what's all this got to do with a limerick?!

DORA. Darling, a limerick has five *lines*, and there were five of *us*. So we each got a single line of it—

JEFF. (*Inspired*.) Wait! I think I've *got* it! Orion's father hid the gold, then made up a limerick that would tell where it was hidden, but gave each of you only a single line of it, so none of you could get at it without the assistance of the others—?!

ROSALIND. Good grief, so *that's* it!

ORION. *Now* do you see why I was so upset at losing my pigeon-thingy?!

BARNSY. "*Jambule*," Orion!

JEFF. You mean—the line from the limerick was *in* it?

ORION. Why, of course!

ROSALIND. What do you mean, "of course"?! There's no of-course *about* it!

DORA. But Rosalind, darling, Great-Grandfather had *drawers* full of those thingies since the last of the pigeons perished, and—

ROSALIND. Do you mean—he wrote the limerick-lines on five of those tiny little rolls of paper they put pigeon-messages on, stuffed them into the whatsies, and passed them out to all of you?

BARNSY. There! Now you've got it! Didn't I *say* it was simple?

JEFF. *No*, you *didn't*!

DORA. I thought *somebody* did . . . ?

ORION. *Father* did.

DORA. Ah, *that's* where I heard it!

JEFF. Stop it! All of you, stop it! Let's get back to the point—

ROSALIND. *What* point?

JEFF. Those limerick-lines—Orion and Barnsy have *lost* theirs, correct?

BARNSY. Not quite, young man.

ROSALIND. You still *have* yours?

BARNSY. Well, no, but I didn't *lose* it—it was taken by force.

ORION. Oh, dash it all, Barnsy, stop being such a pedant! He meant you *had* it, and now you *don't*!

DORA. Then the killer will have *two* clues to the whereabouts of the gold!

JEFF. Probably *three*, now that Cleo's vanished, too!

ROSALIND. But he needs all five! So—

DORA. Well, he shan't get *mine*! I wouldn't *hear* of such a thing!

JEFF. I hope you've kept it in a safe place?

DORA. Of course I have! I very cleverly had it attached to this charm-bracelet! (*Extends wrist toward group.*)

JEFF. *What* charm-bracelet?!

DORA. (*Looks at bare wrist.*) Oh, dear! It must be upstairs in my suitcase!

JEFF. Oh, no! Quickly, everybody—!

(ALL *but* BARBARA—*who, of course, simply stands about trying vaguely to follow matters, to no avail—dash for the stairs and rush up out of sight—*ORION, *with his bad legs, is the last one, of course—and even as he is slowly ascending:*)

BARBARA. Where is everybody *going*? Why does no one *tell* me anything?

MAGNOLIA. (*Enters from kitchen.*) Excuse me, Lady Barbara, but have you seen Medkins?

BARBARA. (*Notices her.*) Oh, Magnolia—have you seen Medkins?

MAGNOLIA. Oh, damn and blast! (*Raises her voice considerably.*) I said—have you seen Medkins?!

BARBARA. Then where *is* he?

MAGNOLIA. *I* just asked *you* that!

BARBARA. Well, will you please go and *fetch* him?

MAGNOLIA. (*Losing patience.*) Lady Barbara—!

BARBARA. Because I'd like a sherry, that's why!

MAGNOLIA. Oh, why don't you get it yourself!

BARBARA. Why, thank you dear, it's kind of you to offer.

MAGNOLIA. (*Gives up.*) Oh, very well, very well! (*Heads for sideboard via downstage route, and* BARBARA *moves that way via upstage route.*) Might as well be talking to the *wall* as try and make *her* understand anything!

BARBARA. Of course, it's really the duty of a *butler* to pour the sherry, but these are difficult times, and I suppose one must make do.

MAGNOLIA. (*At sideboard, now.*) Oh, there's one already poured.

BARBARA. Oh, there's one already poured, so you needn't bother.

MAGNOLIA. (*Impatiently hands her poisoned glass.*) Oh, drink your drink and shut up!

BARBARA. Thank you, my dear. (*Stares at drink.*) My, what a peculiar color!

MAGNOLIA. What's *wrong* with the color?

BARBARA. (*Sniffs at it.*) And such a peculiar odor, too.

MAGNOLIA. Well, I wouldn't know. Never *had* sherry, myself. At *my* wages, I'm lucky to afford a pint of bitters!

BARBARA. Jitters? Yes, I suppose we *all* have them. The murder, you know. It does tend to dampen one's party spirits.

(MAGNOLIA *merely rolls her eyes and shakes her head in exasperation, and* BARBARA *raises the glass to her lips, and the gloved hand pops out of the slot with a pistol, points it ceilingward, and FIRES; neither woman has seen the hand, but both react,* MAGNOLIA *with a loud scream, and* BARBARA *with a jump that lets the glass fall to the floor, as hand swiftly vanishes.*)

BARBARA. What was that noise?

MAGNOLIA. (*Picks up glass, sets it on sideboard during:*) *You* heard it, too? Boy, it *must* have been loud!

BARBARA. Oh, dear, look at this mess on the floor! We must have Medkins clean it up at once!

MAGNOLIA. (*Moves to bell-pull.*) I'll ring for him, mum!

BARBARA. Magnolia, what are you doing! That bell-pull is never to be touched!

(*As* MAGNOLIA *drops her hand from its move toward bell-pull,* JEFF, DORA, BARNSY, ROSALIND *and*

ORION—*last, of course—come rushing down stairs into room, their lines overlapping, on:*)

JEFF. What was that shot?!

DORA. Is anybody hurt?!

BARNSY. What's going on down here?!

DORA. (*Points at spill.*) Look! It's blood!

ROSALIND. *Green* blood?

ORION. Barbara, what's been happening? Are you all right?

MAGNOLIA. She was just having a glass of sherry, and there was a gunshot, and she dropped her glass, but she wouldn't let me ring for Medkins, and—

ORION. Good heavens, girl, you didn't use *that* bell-pull, did you?!

JEFF. Why *shouldn't* she have?

ORION. Father was most strict about it—had me shut up this entire wing after he died, and said I was never to open it again until we were ready to dissolve the tontine!

ROSALIND. But—you *have* opened it! Does that mean—?

(*There is a sudden LTB; ALL scream; then LIGHTS COME UP, and a dazed CLEO is standing where we last saw her, now wearing only a slip.*)

ROSALIND. Cleo! Look, everybody, it's Cleo!

BARBARA. (*As ALL move toward CLEO.*) How *dare* you be seen in your underthings!

BARNSY. (*Squints that way.*) Is she *really*?

CLEO. (*As they gather around her.*) Wait—I can explain—just let me catch my breath—everything happened so fast—!

JEFF. *What* happened?

DORA. Yes, one moment you were here, and the very next moment—

BARNSY. I'll bet it's the very same thing that happened to *me*!

CLEO. Well—the lights went out—

BARNSY. The same! Exactly the same!

CLEO. And someone grabbed me—

BARNSY. Exactly!

CLEO. Flung me down in some dark tunnel or someplace—

BARNSY. The same! The very same!

CLEO. Tore off my dress—

(OTHERS *turn expectantly toward* BARNSY.)

BARNSY. (*Disappointedly.*) There the similarity ends.

CLEO. (*Completing her interrupted narrative.*) Then all at once, I found myself right back *here*! (*Suddenly looks down at herself and realizes:*) Oh! The dirty rat pinched my whatchamacallit!

MAGNOLIA. (*Misunderstanding.*) Oh, go on and *say* it—*we're* all adults here!

CLEO. Say *what*? It was in the pocket of my dress!

MAGNOLIA. Well, *now* I've heard *everything*!

ORION. Oh, *shush*, girl! She's talking about her *thingy*!

MAGNOLIA. Who's *arguing*!?

JEFF. We were right, then! That makes three!

CLEO. What are you talking about?

DORA. There were five of those thingies, and now the killer has all but two!

MAGNOLIA. (*Still at sea.*) *Really*?!

JEFF. Magnolia, will you keep *out* of this?!

DORA. You don't know what we're *talking* about!

MAGNOLIA. (*Shrugs.*) Why should *I* be any different!

ROSALIND. Mag-*no*-lia . . . *shut* . . . *up*!

MAGNOLIA. (*With a toss of her head and a sniff.*) Hmmmph! And they criticize *my* manners! (*Exits huffily to kitchen.*)

JEFF. (*Starts pacing, between hearth and table, as* OTHERS *find new positions:* BARBARA *at sideboard,* ROSALIND *on left settee,* ORION *on right settee,* DORA *on desk chair,* CLEO *leaning against fireplace's right side, and* BARNSY *behind left settee; their moves are accomplished while he speaks:*) We've got to unravel the mystery, and the sooner the better! The whole key to the thing is that tontine and those limerick-lines. I don't suppose— (*Stops pacing, and looks hopefully at* OTHERS.) I don't suppose any of you has *memorized* his or her line—?

CLEO. I'm an actress! Of course I memorized it! Nothing simpler!

JEFF. Thank heaven! How about the rest of you?!

ORION. I'm fairly certain I know mine—it was one of the short ones.

BARNSY. Mine was lengthy, as limericks go, but I do have a good head for poetry.

JEFF. Dora?

DORA. No, I'm afraid not—but it *is* right here in my charm bracelet—! (*Waves wrist from which bracelet now dangles.*) Shall I get it out?

JEFF. Yes, immediately! Then, we'll put the whole thing together and—

CLEO. Hold on! What about *Barbara*?!

(ALL *look with varied degrees of despair toward* BARBARA, *who senses their consensus of despair.*)

BARBARA. Whatever is the *matter* with everyone? You're looking at me as it I'd hiccuped in church!

JEFF. Wait—perhaps the *rest* of you have enough. What are your lines?

(*Over* OTHERS'S *speeches,* DORA *will detach jambule from bracelet, take out rolled paper and unroll it.*)

ORION. Let me see, now—mine was, to the best of my recollection—"They must look for a place . . ."

JEFF. Yes? Go on . . . ?

ORION. That's *it*, old chap!

JEFF. What, are you certain?

CLEO. Perhaps it will make sense among all the *other* lines, Jeff.

JEFF. I most certainly *hope* so! What was *your* line, Cleo?

CLEO. (*Frowns a moment, recalling, then recites slowly:*) "Wants to pull out the gold sugarplums . . ."

ROSALIND. So far, it's gibberish!

JEFF. Well, wait, let's give it a chance. Barnsy—?

BARNSY. "*Miss* Barnsdale," *please*!

ORION. Barnsy, come off it! Our very *lives* may depend on this!

BARNSY. Oh, very well, very well. "When a family that's truly all thumbs . . ."

ROSALIND. What *about* them?

BARNSY. That *all* of it.

JEFF. All of *what*?—Oh, wait, you mean *that* was your part of the *limerick*?

BARNSY. Well, of *course*!

ORION. Damn and blast, woman, you might have *said* so!

JEFF. Could we *please* have it once again?

BARNSY. (*Sighs, then enunciates carefully:*) "When a family that's truly all thumbs . . ." There, are you satisfied?

JEFF. It's *still* not making sense. If only we knew the *order* of the lines—

ORION. Oh, we know *that*, all right.

ROSALIND. You do? How?

ORION. Why, Father *said* he was passing the thingies *out* in order.

JEFF. Aha! And what *was* that order, Mr. Leduc?!

ORION. Why, it was . . . um . . . Barnsy . . . Cleo . . . myself . . . Dora . . . and—Barbara!

ROSALIND. How can you be so certain, dearest?

ORION. Oh, well, as to that—Father said he'd done it that way so we wouldn't forget—do you see—"something old, something new, something borrowed, something blue"—then Barbara.

BARNSY. *What*?! How *dare* he call me old!

ORION. But Barnsy, you *are* the oldest. You were my governess, Cleo's governess, Dora's governess—!

CLEO. But why was *I* "something *new*"?

ORION. Oh, well, you see, you'd just had your first *nose-job*—

CLEO. (*Mortified.*) *Please*, Orion!

ROSALIND. (*Delighted.*) *Nose*-job?! Well, *la-de-da*!

CLEO. Oh, shut your mouth, you little gold-digger!

ROSALIND. "Sticks and stones may break my bones—"

CLEO. Don't *tempt* me!

JEFF. Ladies, please, this is getting us nowhere!

ORION. Jeff's right! Let me finish: The "something borrowed" was my title of baronet, since it wasn't rightfully mine till Father kicked off, but I'd been using it once he seemed to be on his deathbed . . .

JEFF. Mr. Leduc, *how* you memorized the order of bestowals hardly matters—

DORA. Oh, *please* let him finish, Jeff—I want to know why *I* was "something *blue*"! Was it my lovely blue eyes?

ORION. Well, no, my dear, it wasn't. It seems that before you were born, your parents were so sure you'd be a boy that they ordered all the baby clothes in the wrong color!

ROSALIND. But—when she was born, why didn't they make an exchange?!

DORA. Rosalind, that's monstrous!

CLEO. Of the *clothing*, Dora, not of *you*!

JEFF. Listen, all of you—that killer may strike again at any moment—and you're all babbling about baby-clothes and nose-jobs and—

BARNSY. Quite right! We're being foolish! Quickly, now, to the limerick! I'll start: "When a family that's truly all thumbs—"

CLEO. "Wants to pull out the gold sugarplums—"

ORION. "They must look for a place—"

DORA. (*Reading from unrolled paper:*) "Showing my smiling *colon*—!

CLEO. (*Nearly gags.*) *Yucch*! That's absolutely *disgusting*!

BARNSY. And a *terrible* rhyme!

JEFF. Darling, are you *sure* that's what it says?

DORA. (*Scans paper again, then brightens.*) Oh, *now* I see! I hadn't unfolded this one little bit—There! Ah, *now* it makes sense! (*Nods, starts to re-roll paper and put it into* jambule.)

OTHERS. (*Except* BARBARA.) (*Any sitters coming to their feet as they shout:*) *What does it say*?!

DORA. (*Comes to her own feet, on:*) Well, I *can't* read it *now*—the *rhythm* will be spoiled!

JEFF. Dora, for the love of heaven—!

CLEO. Jeff, let's do it *her* way. It's always best to humor a nut!

DORA. Who are you calling a nut?!

CLEO. If the straitjacket *fits*—!

ROSALIND. All right, all right! Let's take it from the top! . . . Barnsy—?

(*Next three speeches are said mechanically, with resignation.*)

BARNSY. "When a family that's truly all thumbs—"

CLEO. "Wants to pull out the gold sugarplums—"

ORION. "They must look for a place—"

DORA. (*Reads carefully.*) "Showing my smiling face . . . *colon!*"

ROSALIND. Make up your mind! Is it *face* or *colon*?!

DORA. Face. *Followed* by a colon.

JEFF. Aha! That means that the *final* line tells us *where* the gold *is*!

(ALL *turn hopefully toward* BARBARA.)

BARBARA. What's the matter? Why are you all staring at me that way?

ORION. It's no use. She hasn't the foggiest notion what's going on! We'll have to write it down for her!

DORA. (*Starts rummaging in desk drawers.*) I *know* there's half a pencil in here *someplace* . . . ! Let me see, now—ink—stapler—ruler—rubberbands—eraser—paperweight—

MAGNOLIA. (*Rushes in from kitchen carrying a broom, stops between bench and hearth.*) I've found Medkins! He came back just as I was sweeping up!

CLEO. *I* didn't know he was *lost!*

BARBARA. Ah, Magnolia! Have you found Medkins yet?

MAGNOLIA. Yes, mum, I have!

JEFF. Just a moment—why were you *looking* for him?

MAGNOLIA. Because he disappeared so mysteriously, sir.

ROSALIND. What? When?

MAGNOLIA. When we were putting away the dinner dishes, mum. He stepped into the pantry, and when I looked inside, he was gone!

ORION. But when *exactly* was that?

MAGNOLIA. Just shortly before that mysterious gunshot that made Lady Barbara spill her poisoned drink.

BARNSY. What? Her drink was poisoned? How do you know?

MAGNOLIA. Well, I *didn't* know—not at the *time*—but I recognized the *color* of the poison—a rather nasty shade of green.

JEFF. But Magnolia—if you know the color of the poison—why didn't you know it at the time she spilled her drink?

MAGNOLIA. I thought it was just some sort of *sauce*, sir.

BARBARA. You've broken a *saucer*? Oh, dear! I hope it wasn't the good china!

ORION. Barbara, shut up!

BARBARA. Hmm?

DORA. (*She and* ALL BUT BARBARA *are now converging upon* MAGNOLIA.) Magnolia, you're not making sense. What has the poison got to do with Medkins' disappearance?

MAGNOLIA. Well, when I went into the kitchen, just now, he was just coming out of the pantry, carrying a small bottle—or perhaps a flask—no, it was too small for that—maybe a vial—

ROSALIND. Just say "container" and get on with your story!

MAGNOLIA. Yes, mum. Container. And it was filled with the green poison.

CLEO. Look, you're *still* not making sense. So you saw a bottle, and the bottle was filled with a green liquid, and it's the same liquid you think was dumped into Barbara's drink—you *still* haven't explained how you know it's *poison*!

MAGNOLIA. Oh, well, as to that—it's the same sort of stuff he poured on all the horse's doovers!

ORION. *Hors d'oeuvre*!

MAGNOLIA. Sorry, sir.

JEFF. He poisoned the *hors d'oeuvre*? How can you be so certain?

MAGNOLIA. Because, sir—I just *ate* one. (*She immediately rolls up her eyes, and falls into the arms of the group, who lay her down on the floor, during:*)

ORION. Good heavens!

CLEO. She's dead!

ROSALIND. Murdered!

BARNSY. Right before our very eyes!

DORA. It's horrible! Horrible!

BARBARA. (*Picks up broom.*) Such an *untidy* girl!

JEFF. Wait! Look there on the floor beside her! Plaster-dust!

CLEO. (*Looks ceilingward.*) There! In the ceiling!

ROSALIND. (*Looks.*) Is that a bullet-hole?!

ORION. Do you suppose that shot we heard earlier—?

DORA. But—why would the killer fire a bullet into the ceiling?

JEFF. (*Snaps his fingers.*) I've *got* it! It's all starting to make sense, now! For all we know—(*Points dramatically toward* [*imaginary, of course*] *plaster-dust on floor beside* MAGNOLIA.) In that tiny mound of plaster-dust lies the key that may well unlock the solution of this entire mystery!

BARBARA. (*Looks where he is pointing, and instantly and efficiently, with a one-two back-and-forth sweep of the broom, clears the* [*imaginary*] *spot;* OTHERS *react with horror, but even as they do, she looks up and remarks apologetically:*) Good servants are *so* hard to get!

(*And as they all just stand there, staring at her—.*)

## THE CURTAIN FALLS

## ACT THREE

*Shortly before dawn. Garden doors are open wide, but
all is still blackness outside.* JEFF *is half-seated on
edge of desk, facing into room, holding pistol;* BAR-
BARA *is seated at lower end of left settee, engrossed
in reading a lurid mystery magazine, its cover visible to us;* ORION *is at sideboard, pouring himself a
glass of sherry;* BARNSY *is seated at lower end of
right settee, holding her left shoe in left hand, while
right hand massages stockinged left foot, which she
has ankle-rested on right knee;* DORA *is at hearth,
toasting a marshmallow on a stick [a small bowl of
more of the marshmallows is at table's center];*
ROSALIND *is lounging on bench, her legs along its
length downstageward, arms very firmly folded,
her expression mingling irritation and weariness,
but we can see that it is Side #2 of the bench that is
in view [since the backside of portrait figure(s) is in
view], despite our last view of it having been Side
#1. After a moment:*

DORA. Darling, are you *sure* I can't toast you a
marshmallow? (*Will remove her [pre-toasted] marshmallow from stick and happily chew and swallow it,
during:*)
JEFF. Dora, how can you eat marshmallows at a time
like this?!
BARNSY. (*Squints toward voice.*) Would you rather
she ran about the room shrieking? (*Will restore her shoe
to her foot, during:*)
ORION. Don't give her ideas!

ROSALIND. Orion, darling, how *can* you calmly help yourself to *sherry*, after two attempts at *poisoning* people!

ORION. Rosalind, I can see the color of it perfectly well. Not green at all.

DORA. But what if Medkins has switched to *colorless* poison?

ORION. (*Stops glass just short of lips.*) Damn and blast! (*Sets glass back on sideboard, untasted.*)

JEFF. I *wish* the police would get here! I can barely keep my eyes open.

DORA. (*Sets empty stick on table, moves toward him.*) Then why don't you take a nice *nap*, darling?

ROSALIND. Because he might not wake up alive.

BARNSY. The way my feet feel, sudden death might be a blessing. These shoes weren't built for all-night pacing.

ORION. Then go barefoot, Barnsy. Nobody would mind.

BARNSY. *I* would mind. If I *must* die, I shall do it with decorum!

ROSALIND. (*Stretches, stands, during:*) But where *are* the police?! It's nearly dawn. They should have been here *hours* ago!

DORA. (*Now beside* JEFF, *her hand fondly on his arm.*) Perhaps they've missed their way in the dark.

BARNSY. Dora, I know this is a small village, but the police cars *do* have *headlights*!

ORION. Of course, the new police station is at the far end of the village.

JEFF. (*Stands.*) Even so, the village is scarcely a mile wide! They could have *walked* here by *now*!

BARNSY. It *is* odd, the more I think of it. Orion, did they give any indication of a delay when you rang them up?

ORION. Matter of fact, I *didn't* ring them up. I was

too busy helping Jeffrey carry Barnaby's body upstairs.
I asked *Rosalind* to call them.

ROSALIND. Yes, but I was too busy helping Cleo get
over her hysterics. I asked *Dora* to call them.

DORA. But *I* was busy helping Magnolia clean up the
glasses and things about the room.

JEFF. You mean you never *called* them?!

DORA. (*Laughs prettily.*) Now, Jeff, would *I* overlook
an important thing like *that*?

OTHERS. (*Always minus* BARBARA, *of course.*) (*In
unison.*) Yes!

DORA. (*Startled.*) Well, I *didn't*, so there!

BARNSY. Didn't *overlook* it, or didn't *call* them?!

DORA. Didn't *overlook* it, of course!

JEFF. (*Relieved.*) Then you *did* phone the police!

DORA. Well . . . no.

OTHERS. (*In unison.*) Then *what*?!

DORA. Why, I asked *Medkins* to call them!

(OTHERS *react with varied degrees of groaning; then:*)

ROSALIND. Dora, you dunce, Medkins is the murderer!

DORA. (*Defensively.*) Well, I didn't *know* that *then*!

JEFF. But once you *did* know, why didn't you *tell* us!

DORA. Because we all found out at the same *time*,
darling. There was no need.

ORION. *Not* about him being a *killer*, you lunatic!

BARNSY. About him not phoning for the *police*!

DORA. Well, now, we can't be *certain* he didn't phone
them.

OTHERS. (*In unison.*) Why *not*?!

DORA. Because he hadn't been exposed as the
murderer yet, and calling the police would be a part of
his *cover*, do you see?

(OTHERS *groan, shaking their heads.*)

JEFF. (*Grabbing up phone.*) I'd better call them right now! (*Listens at phone, jiggles hook, frowns.*) That's funny—the phone's dead.

BARNSY. That's not the *least bit* funny!

JEFF. (*Slams phone down.*) I didn't mean *that* kind of "funny"!

DORA. Don't worry, darling. At least we have *you* here.

ORION. I'd rather we had the *police*!

DORA. Well, he *is* a police *reporter*. It's practically the same thing!

BARNSY. (*Stands.*) Nonsense! It's not even close!

ROSALIND. Police *arrest* criminals—reporters only *write* about it!

DORA. Well, at least he has a pistol.

ORION. That reminds me—where did you *get* the pistol, anyhow?

JEFF. It was in the desk. These overstuffed drawers hold nearly anything a person could want.

DORA. Except a pen. (*Abruptly cheery.*) Oh! Do you know, that's given me an *idea*!

ROSALIND. There's a first time for everything.

BARNSY. Rosalind, there is no need to be rude.

ORION. Dora isn't *totally* stupid, you know.

ROSALIND. (*Dryly.*) She merely asked the murderer to fetch the police!

(*Any further colloquy is interrupted, however, as* CLEO—*now in another dress, carrying her suitcases, enters via stairs.*)

ORION. Cleo! Leaving so soon?

CLEO. It can't be soon enough for *me*! *I'm* not sticking around to be the *next* victim!

DORA. Oh, but you shouldn't carry your own bags—you should ask a servant.

ROSALIND. *Which* servant—the killer or the corpse?

JEFF. Say—that reminds me—what's become of Magnolia's body?

ORION. Why—we laid her down right over there, on that bench.

BARNSY. (*Squints.*) She's *gone*? I could have *sworn* I saw a corpse lying there.

ROSALIND. That was me!

BARNSY. "That was *I*!"

DORA. They're *both* corpses?!

JEFF. Say, I just noticed—there's something very peculiar about that picture! Shouldn't she [*Or he, or they, as the case may be.*] be facing the other way?

ORION. Now that you mention it—she [*or etc.*] *does* seem to be *backward*!

CLEO. Well, she wouldn't stick out like a sore thumb in *this* group! (*Starts toward hall with bags.*)

JEFF. Wait! You can't go—not yet!

CLEO. (*Pauses in archway.*) You just *watch* me!

JEFF. But we need your Bentley!

CLEO. What for?

ORION. To go fetch the police.

CLEO. You mean they won't come unless you *drive* them?

ROSALIND. Cleo, you don't understand. The phone is dead, and it turns out that dopey little Dora never called them at all.

DORA. But I *did* ask *Medkins* to do so.

CLEO. *Medkins*?! She's not dopey—she's demented! I'm getting *out* of here! (*Turns to depart, but:*)

DORA. Could you at least stop by the police station on your way?

CLEO. Listen, honey, when I go out those doors, I am putting my foot down on the accelerator and keeping it there till I'm safe in my own bed!

ROSALIND. Wouldn't you know she'd have a drive-in bedroom!

CLEO. (*Drops suitcases, starts for* ROSALIND, *fingers like claws.*) I've had about enough out of you—!

ROSALIND. (*Takes boxer's stance.*) Put 'em up! Come on, put 'em up!

JEFF. (*Manages to stop* CLEO's *approach between bench and settee.*) Hold on, now, hold on!

CLEO. (*Melts in his grasp.*) I'm holding, darling!

DORA. How dare you call him that!

CLEO. (*Reluctantly eases out of* JEFF's *arms.*) I'm a *movie* star—I call *everybody* "darling".

ROSALIND. Well, we're back to the drive-in bedroom again!

CLEO. At least *I* don't have to *marry* for money!

ORION. Don't talk rot, Cleo. Why, Rosalind said *she'd* have me if I were *penniless*!

CLEO. Have you *shot*, maybe!

JEFF. Ladies, ladies! Can you hold your chitchat till we've solved this crime?!

CLEO. We *have* solved it: The *butler* did it!

BARNSY. Ah, but he's not *really* a butler!

DORA. He *can't* be a *maid*—?!

JEFF. Barnsy—

BARNSY. "*Miss* Barnsdale"!

DORA. Why are you so insistent on being known as a *miss*?

BARNSY. (*Thinks it over.*) She has a point. (*To* JEFF.) You may call me "Barnsy."

JEFF. Thank you. Now, what I was about to ask you, is—

CLEO. Look, can you just *mail* me the solution to the crime? My Bentley is about to flee, and I'd like to be in it when it does.

JEFF. (*Stops her before she can turn completely*

*away.*) Cleo—I hate to say this, but—there's a very good reason why you can't leave just yet.

CLEO. (*Turns back.*) What reason?

JEFF. (*Awkwardly.*) Well, you see, Barnaby *did* say there were *two* imposters in this house. We know that Medkins is *one* of them, but—well—

CLEO. (*Amazed.*) *I* might be the *other*?

JEFF. *Anyone* might be!

DORA. Except *me*, of course.

JEFF. (*Even more awkwardly.*) Well, as to that—

ORION. What, you suspect your own fiancee?!

DORA. Jeff, how could you!

JEFF. It's only—well—there are a lot of very shaky statements have been made here this evening—and I'm afraid *you* made *one* of them.

CLEO. Say, now, this may be worth sticking around for, after all! (*Will move to desk chair and sit, during:*) I'd like very much to *hear* what she said.

DORA. (*Huffily.*) And so would I! (*Moves to sit beside* BARNSY, *who now sits down again, and* ROSALIND *reclaims her place on bench once more.*)

JEFF. (*Now between right settee and desk.*) All right. It's just this: When Barnaby wrote his B-A-R on that paper, you immediately suggested it stood for Rosalind Barstow—that you'd *never* trusted her.

ROSALIND. (*Insulted.*) Well, *I* like *that*!

DORA. (*Twists—downstagely—to semi-face her.*) I'm *so* glad you're not upset! (*Then, to* JEFF:) But darling—why *shouldn't* I have said that?

JEFF. Because, darling, until tonight—if I understand matters correctly—you and Rosalind had never even *met*.

ORION. Aha!

JEFF. On the other hand, Mr. Leduc, you and Rosalind claimed to have spent the time of Barnaby's murder strolling in the garden—but you didn't.

CLEO. Aha!

JEFF. And *you* claimed to be dawdling over dinner!

BARNSY. Aha!

JEFF. And *you* pretended to be reading wine-cellar labels!

BARBARA. Aha! (OTHERS, *startled, look her way in amazement, but she is just looking up from magazine, and points at page, on:*) *Lord Havisham* put the cobra in the punchbowl! I knew it all the time! (*Drops magazine on table, folds arms in triumph.*)

JEFF. (*Manages to get back on the track.*) And finally, we have Lady Barbara's supposed *nap* during the murder.

DORA. Well, we can *hardly* ask *her* about it!

CLEO. *Oh*, yes we can! (*Will take paper and half-pencil from desk, during:*) I'm going right over there and write every last thing *down* for her to *see!* We're going to get to the bottom of things! (*Will move to sit upstage of* BARBARA *on left settee, during:*)

JEFF. Thank you, Cleo. I appreciate the favor.

CLEO. Why, Jeff, honey, *I* have favors I haven't even *used* yet! (*Flashes him a sultry smile.*)

BARNSY. Now, that *is* funny!

(*During following sequence,* CLEO *will "write things down" busily, "following events," and will show page to* BARBARA *each time it is* BARBARA'S *time to make a reply to anything.*)

JEFF. All right, now—let's have it—what are the *true* stories you all have to tell?! (*Explanations come so fast they almost overlap:*)

DORA. I *already* didn't trust Rosalind *before* I met her because Aunt Barbara *wrote* me of her in her semi-monthly *letters!*

ORION. And Rosalind and I weren't in the garden because—

ROSALIND. —we were under the terrace-overhang smooching!

CLEO. And I left the dining table to go to the. bathroom, but I was too shy to tell anyone!

BARNSY. And I went into the cellar because I thought I was taking the passageway back here, but was too embarrassed to admit I don't see very well!

BARBARA. And I went upstairs to take off my corset because it was killing me, but was too much of a lady to admit it!

JEFF. (*Dashed.*) Oh. Well. I guess that rather *does* account for matters, doesn't it!

DORA. Don't be *too* downhearted, darling. After all, this *is* your first case.

CLEO. Now, Jeff, darling, don't fret—there are still oodles of things that require explanation!

ROSALIND. Such as?

CLEO. (*Ticking items off on her fingers.*) Why was that bullet fired into the ceiling? Why would Medkins poison the *hors d'oeuvre* when he hadn't yet learned Lady Barbara's line of the limerick? Why did Orion invite us all here in the first place? How can Barbara's last name be "Fenwick" if she's the widow of Mr. Leduc's *brother*? How could Barnaby's name be "Folcey" if he's the *son* of Orion's *only* brother? And if he is, doesn't that make him *Barbara's* son, *too*? And finally, what was the "fascinating notion" that popped into Barnsy's head just before she vanished?

JEFF. (*A bit overwhelmed.*) Uh—how many puzzles does *that* make?

ORION. *I* make it *seven*!

DORA. Oh, no, Uncle, there were seven *questions*, so *you* make it *eight*!

ORION. Dammit, Dora, *I'm* not a puzzle!

CLEO. Only as regards his taste in women!

ROSALIND. Now, listen, you middle-aged man-trap—!

BARNSY. Hold it! *First* let's solve the murders—*then* you can kill one another.

JEFF. Right! Now, let's take the questions in order: Why was that bullet fired into the ceiling?

CLEO. To startle Barbara into spilling her poisoned drink, because the killer wanted her alive till he learned her limerick-line.

JEFF. But then, why would he poison the *hors d'oeuvre*? *That* might have done her in—?!

BARBARA. But *hors d'oeuvre* are all ham and anchovies and caviar and I'm on a salt-free diet!

JEFF. Ah, it's all beginning to make sense!

DORA. Not to *me*!

ROSALIND. So what *else* is new?

JEFF. Now, why did Orion invite all of you here in the first place?

ORION. My motives were entirely selfish: Times are hard, taxes are up, and the tontine was the only possible source of money for me!

JEFF. So you needed the remaining four lines of the limerick!

BARNSY. *That* makes sense!

DORA. Not to *me*!

ROSALIND. No comment.

JEFF. Okay, so far so good. Now, how can Barbara's surname be "Fenwick" if she's married to a Leduc?

BARBARA. He was only my *first* husband. My *second* was a *Fenwick*.

JEFF. But how could Barnaby's surname be "Folcey" if *he* were the son of that *same* Leduc?

BARBARA. Ah, that was by my late *husband's* first marriage. He had married a Folcey girl, and she insisted the child be surnamed after *her*!

JEFF. And your husband *agreed*?

BARBARA. (*Shrugs.*) She never *told* him.

DORA. Oh, how marvelously *simple*!

ROSALIND. You sure are!

JEFF. That brings us to the final puzzle: Barnsy, just what *was* the notion that popped into your head before you vanished?

BARNSY. (*Thinks.*) Let me see—it had something to do with Barbara—with her acting-classes. (*Shakes her head.*) No—no, I'm sorry—it went quite out of my head when I was grabbed and robbed of my *jambule*! Perhaps I'll think of it later.

CLEO. (*Stands.*) Well, if that takes care of all the mysteries, I'll just be hitting the road! (*Heads to desk, where she'll leave paper and half-pencil.*)

DORA. Wait, there's still *one* more minor mystery— *whatever* became of Magnolia's *body*?

JEFF. That *is* a puzzling thing! (*Moves toward bench.*) Now, we left her right there—and I'll swear she was dead—but I also know that nobody had a chance to carry her away, so—?

ORION. (*Shuffling benchward—and he moves so slowly, it's best if he starts the move on* DORA'S *preceding line.*) Oh, as to that, it's on some sort of turn-table—swivels about into the wall if you press the right spot on the bench-arm.

CLEO. What?! Orion, why didn't you tell us before?!

ORION. (*Nearing bench, now.*) Didn't *know* about it until it *happened* to me!

BARNSY. (*Rising and moving after him toward bench.*) Do you mean—you vanished *yourself*? I mean, the *killer* didn't do it?

DORA. But how *could* he have? Medkins was right in the room when it occurred.

ROSALIND. I don't believe it!

DORA. That Medkins was in the room?

ROSALIND. That you made a sensible statement!

JEFF. (*As* ALL *but still-seated* BARBARA *converge near bench.*) Mr. Leduc—when you accidentally triggered the mechanism and rotated into the wall—what happened then?

ORION. It's kind of fuzzy—I was in a dark passage, and I started wandering about trying to find my way out—then someone hit me over the head and tied me up—and finally popped me back out into this room.

JEFF. (*Sits on bench.*) Then there's only one thing to do—I'd better go *in* there and try to find Medkins!

CLEO. But what if he's *not* in there?

DORA. Why, then, Jeff will come back *out*, of course! *Won't* you, darling!

JEFF. *If* I can figure out how to *move* this thing—! (*Feels arm of bench.*) Wait—I think I feel the starting-stud—*Whoops*!

(*This last shout is because bench rotates him into wall, exposing Side #1, but no sign of* MAGNOLIA.)

DORA. (*Points at empty bench.*) There ought to be a *body* there!

ROSALIND. Boy, you'd make a lousy interior decorator!

CLEO. Hey—I just thought—Jeff has our only weapon! If Medkins should come back here right *now*—!?

(ALL [*but* BARBARA] *panic, and* DORA *rushes to phone,* BARNSY *rushes to blank face of right hearth wall, and* ORION *starts his geisha-shuffle toward left archway, as each says:*)

DORA. *I'll* call for the *police*! (*Has phone—remember, it's the old-fashioned kind, with earpiece on a hook, and mouthpiece on a stand—held to her ear and mouth—but the mouthpiece to her ear, and the earpiece to her mouth—as she continues:*) Hello? . . . *Hello?* . . . HELLO?

BARNSY. (*Leaning forward, squinting at blank wall of hearth.*) And I'll keep a lookout for the killer!

ORION. (*Shuffling away.*) And I'll run for help!

CLEO. *Hold* it, *all* of you! (DORA *hangs up,* BARNSY *turns, and* ORION *stops, during:*) I think maybe I'd better drive to the police station, after all! It's our only hope!

ROSALIND. (*As* CLEO *passes* ORION *en route to archway.*) Wait, I'd better come with you—you don't know the location of the new police station!

CLEO. (*Has continued to archway, picked up her bags.*) Aren't you afraid we'll tear each other's hair out?

ROSALIND. (*Arriving at archway.*) It beats getting stabbed!

CLEO. You've *got* something there!

(BOTH *exit to front hall.*)

DORA. (*As* ORION, *wheezing from his exertions, sinks down onto settee opposite* BARBARA.) It's *so* nice to be *home* again! Nothing this exciting *ever* happens in *Delaware!*

BARNSY. (*Snaps her fingers in triumph.*) That's *it*! That's the thing I forgot when I got grabbed!

DORA. How dull it is in Delaware?

BARNSY. (*Moves to position upstage of table, while* DORA *moves to position just behind* ORION.) No-no! *Barnaby,* I mean! He was supposed to have lived all these years in America—yet he'd never heard of *Dover,* its capital!

DORA. Oh! And he didn't know his nickname was "Wartsy," *either,* come to think of it!

BARNSY. And just before he died, he told you there were *two* imposters at this party!

ORION. Great Godfrey! You don't mean—?!

BARNSY. *He* was *one* of them!

ORION. And *Medkins* was the *other!*

DORA. Oh, how *clever* you are! (*Turns and rushes to bench.*) I *must* tell Jeff the good news! (*Leans over bench, fumbling at one of its arms.*) How do you *work* this thing, anyway? . . . Oh, wait, *I've* got it—! (*Pushes stud, then leaps backward away from bench as it rotates to Side #2 again—because* MEDKINS, *gun in hand, is seated smilingly on it.*) What *is* this! *You're* not Jeff!

BARNSY. (*Squinting that way.*) *Who* isn't?

DORA. (*Turns her way, disappointed.*) Oh, it's only Medkins! (*Then realizes, popeyed:*) *Medkins!*

ORION. (*Jumps to his feet, turns benchward.*) It *is* Medkins!

BARBARA. (*Comes out of her normal bemusement, sees him.*) Oh, Medkins, might I trouble you for a glass of sherry—?

MEDKINS. (*Stands, gun-waving* DORA *to back up from him toward* BARNSY.) I think *not,* Lady Barbara.

BARBARA. Hmm?

MEDKINS. (*To* DORA *and* BARNSY.) Both of you—over there and sit! (BOTH *move to settees,* BARNSY *near* BARBARA, DORA *near* ORION, *as* MEDKINS *moves to spot upstage of table, gun-menacing them.*) And keep your hands where I can see them!

(DORA, BARNSY *and* ORION *sit, very nervous:* BARBARA, *of course, still smiles at them all in sweet befuddlement.*)

BARBARA. Then how about some *gin?*

MEDKINS. (*Leans toward her across table, his headside in* DORA'S *range.*) Now, listen to me, you old foof—!

DORA. (*Gasps, pointing toward his ear.*) *WARTSY!*

MEDKINS. (*Straightens at once, startled, his hand going guiltily to his ear for a moment.*) Don't be ridiculous!

DORA. But I *know* those warts! All three of them! You're not Medkins at all! You're Cousin Barnaby!

[*NOTE: For purposes of non-confusion of character— players, we will continue to call* MEDKINS *by phony name.*]

BARNSY. So that's it! The answer to the puzzle! We never *could* figure out why anyone would bump off *Barnaby*—and now we know: Nobody *did!*

ORION. But then—who *was* that other chap who got murdered?

MEDKINS. An actor. I hired him to pose as me for the duration of the party. When he suspected my motives, well—I had to kill him, that's all.

BARNSY. But if you're Barnaby—why did the person Orion called at the agency say they were sending a "Medkins" to us?

MEDKINS. That wasn't a domestics agent—that was *another* actor I hired to *pose* as one!

ORION. But, dash it all, your *credentials*, man! I mean, you were driven to my door in an agency *automobile!*

MEDKINS. Driven by *another* actor I hired to pose as a chauffeur!

DORA. But Barnaby, what was the *point* of it all?!

BARNSY. Yes, you certainly seem to have over-complicated things excessively!

MEDKINS. What other choice did I have? If I came here as *myself*, and murdered you all, I'd be the prime suspect, and probably be *hanged* before I could inherit. But as a *dead* person, once the *substitute* Barnaby was out of the way under *my name*, I'd never be suspected at all!

ORION. You're *still* not making sense! If the police thought you were *dead*, even if you *did* murder us all, there'd be no way for you to *get* the inheritance!

MEDKINS. Ah, but I thought of that, too, and wisely made out a *will*, so that—being thought dead—*my* heir would get all the money!

DORA. *What* heir?

MEDKINS. A man called Joshua Frobisher, who lives in faraway Phoenix.

BARNSY. But what good would that do *you*?

MEDKINS. Don't you understand? *I* am that Joshua Frobisher!

ORION. But wouldn't you be recognized when you came to collect the cash?

MEDKINS. No, because I would simply hire *another* actor to collect *for* me!

DORA. Boy, *Equity* would be just *crazy* about *you*!

BARNSY. But Barnaby—if that *was* your plan—why *haven't* you murdered us all?

MEDKINS. Because of the blasted *tontine*! There *was* no money for me to inherit, I learned shortly after I arrived, yesterday. Not until those five limerick-lines were put together, and the whereabouts of the gold discovered! I had to let you all live until I learned them!

ORION. I say! I've just realized something! Since those two imposters that Barnaby—that is, that *actor* you hired—the two imposters he tried to name were *you* and *himself*, it means that—

BARNSY. —when he was dying, and they asked him to write the name of his killer, and he wrote the letters B-A-R—!

MEDKINS. (*Shrugs.*) He was trying to spell out "*Barnaby*"!

DORA. "Barnaby"! B-A-R stood for "Barnaby"! We

never even *considered* he might be writing his *own* name!

BARNSY. Even if he'd *completed* the name, we'd be more confused than *ever*!

ORION. Except Dora. I'm afraid she's already reached her limit.

DORA. Now-now, Uncle Orion, this is no time for compliments!

ORION. Oh, never mind that! The important thing is—just what do you intend doing with us, *now*, Medkins— oh, I mean, Barnaby.

MEDKINS. Why, get the last line of the limerick from Lady Barbara, murder you all, take the gold, and live happily ever after!

DORA. You won't get away with it! Any moment now, Jeff will come back here, and—

(*At that moment,* JEFF—*ankles and wrists tied—comes hopping into room via cellar access, a loosened handkerchief-gag dangling about his neck, on:*)

JEFF. Dora! Everybody! I've solved the case! The killer is *Barnaby*! (*Stops, seeing* MEDKINS.) Oh, drat.

DORA. (*Rushes to him.*) My poor darling! Did he hurt you?! (*Will start to undo his bonds.*)

MEDKINS. Here, now, keep away from him!

BARNSY. Oh, don't be such a grouch, Barnaby! What's the sense of worrying whether he's tied up or not if you plan to shoot him anyway?!

MEDKINS. Well, I daresay you're right— (*Suddenly realizes.*) Say, what's become of Cleo and Rosalind?!

DORA. Oh, *they've* just gone to fetch the *police*.

MEDKINS. *What*?!

DORA. (*Turning from a now-freed* JEFF.) Now, now, you needn't worry. You can murder us all and make your getaway in plenty of time.

JEFF. *Dora!*

DORA. But he *can*, darling!

JEFF. You shouldn't have even *told* him where they'd *gone!*

DORA. But, Jeff, he was bound to find out—once he saw the Bentley was gone—

MEDKINS. The Bentley?! Now, *that's* a relief!

BARNSY. (*Sensing his elation.*) Oh, you wicked man, what have you done?!

MEDKINS. Gimmicked the brakes on the Bentley—the first curve in the road they come to, they'll plunge to their deaths in the sea!

DORA. Oh, Barnaby, that was *naughty* of you!

JEFF. *If* you care to put it *mildly!*

ORION. (*Wringing his hands.*) Oh, what shall we do, what shall we do, we're doomed, doomed, doomed!

DORA. *I* have it! Let's stall for time! (*To* MEDKINS.) Lovely weather we're having—! (*There is an instant THUNDERCLAP outside; as it dies, she adds, lamely:*) —for England.

MEDKINS. Now, Dora, if you will kindly return to your seat—

DORA. (*As she and* JEFF *move setteeward.*) So, you're the killer, Barnaby! How terribly devious of you! (*Thoughtful.*) And all because of a mere fortune in gold! (*Curious.*) But it is absolutely necessary to *kill* us all?

JEFF. Dora, must you *remind* him of that?!

DORA. (*In loud whisper which* ALL *can hear.*) I'm still stalling for *time*, darling! Why don't *you* take a try at it?

JEFF. But what good would *that* do?! If Cleo and Rosalind *were* getting the police, it would make sense, but with the car's brakes gimmicked—!

DORA. But a policeman *might* drop *by!*

JEFF. Dora, you are a total *nincompoop!*

DORA. (*Turns away from him, huffily.*) *Oh*, stick it in your ear!

ORION. Dora! Where did you learn such language!

DORA. From Great-Grandfather Farlow, of course!

BARNSY. Yes, Orion, he spoke like that to everyone who annoyed him!

DORA. I'll never forget the day we got our limerick-lines from him!

ORION. Nor will I! He got absolutely *furious* at *Barbara*!

BARNSY. But who could *blame* the man! She was a nervous wreck, clutching her little *jambule*, and continually piping "Where shall I *hide* it, where shall I *hide* it, where shall I *hide* it?!" until we were *all* ready to scream!

DORA. Yes, it's no *wonder* he told her to stick it in her ear!

(*Two beats, ALL immobile; then ALL realize at once, on:*)

ALL BUT BARBARA. *Stick it in her ear!*

JEFF. So *that's* it!

ORION. It *must* be it!

BARNSY. It's *got* to be it!

DORA. Of *course* it's it!

MEDKINS. But—you mean she *actually* stuck it in her ear?!—That's *crazy*!

JEFF. In *this* family, who'd *notice*!

MEDKINS. Orion—how *long* has Lady Barbara been hard of hearing?

ORION. Why—from the day Father passed away—!

DORA. Oh! Do you suppose—?!

BARNSY. And here, *we* all thought is was the shock of his *death*!

ORION. *What* shock? He was ninety-seven years old!

DORA. Still and all, it must have been a shock to *him*!

(*At this moment,* CLEO *and* ROSALIND, *their clothing in rags and tatters, lurch in via garden doors.*)

JEFF. Cleo! Rosalind! You're not dead!

MEDKINS. But—the Bentley—I gimmicked the brakes!

BARNSY. Not well *enough*, apparently.

CLEO. Oh, *he* did a *dandy* job!

DORA. Then how did you *stop*?

ROSALIND. We ran smack into Barnsy's cottage!

JEFF. Before you got up to highway speed! How lucky for you!

BARNSY. Where did the car stop, in my rock garden or my peony bush?

CLEO. Your living room!

BARNSY. Oh, no! And I just had the carpet cleaned!

ORION. You fools! Why did you come back *here*?!

DORA. Medkins plans to kill us all! I mean, Barnaby.

ROSALIND. But—he's *already* killed Barnaby!

MEDKINS. Not quite. You see—*I* am Barnaby!

CLEO. *You* are?

ROSALIND. Then who *was* murdered?

MEDKINS. I'm *not* going to go through all *that* again!

DORA. We'll explain it all after the killer is captured.

MEDKINS. Oh, Dora, shut up! Now, you two, get over here where I can see you! (CLEO *and* ROSALIND *move to rear of right settee and stand there, opposite* JEFF, *who stands behind left settee since* DORA *took her seat again.*) And now, Lady Barbara, lend me your ear!

BARBARA. Hmm? (*Then, as he "grabs jambule from within her ear" [actually making the motion with an already-palmed jambule]:*) Oh! Stop! What are you doing!

MEDKINS. (*Clumsily unfolding paper from within jambule, juggling gun a bit as he does so.*) Finding out the secret of the final limerick-line at last! (*Looks at paper.*) Aha! So *that's* it!

CLEO. You know the location of the *gold*?

MEDKINS. Not quite.

JEFF. Why not?

MEDKINS. Because I forget the *first* four lines!

DORA. Oh, goody, let's not *tell* him!

ROSALIND. But he's *got* all the *other* jambules!

DORA. (*Extends charm bracelet.*) Not *mine*, he hasn't! (*He grabs it off her wrist.*) . . . Hadn't.

MEDKINS. (*Realizes impossibility of juggling-reading-menacing all at once.*) Let's save time. Just *recite* your lines for me, please!

DORA. (*Stands.*) After the rude way you yanked that off my wrist?!

MEDKINS. It's *nothing* compared to the rude way I'll shoot you in the *foot*!

JEFF. Better not argue with him.

DORA. (*Taking a backstep toward bench.*) Who's arguing! My line is—

MEDKINS. Wait! In order, please! And no tricks!

BARNSY. (*Sighs, but starts.*) "When a family that's truly all thumbs—"

CLEO. "Wants to pull out the gold sugarplums—"

ORION. "They must look for a place—"

DORA. "Showing my smiling face—" (MEDKINS, *elated, starts to read final line, but she adds:*) "*Colon*—!"

MEDKINS. (*Glares at her, then reads final line:*) "With a tug of the cord, down it comes!"

ROSALIND. *What* smiling face?

BARBARA. *What* cord? (*Brightens.*) Oh! I heard him! I'm cured! I can hear, I can hear! (*She is on her feet by final word.*) I've come back to the wonderful world of sound!

MEDKINS. Then *listen*, Auntie: One more peep out of you and I'll *plug* you!

BARBARA. (*Glumly.*) Some comeback! (*Sits again.*)

MEDKINS. Now, quickly! Tell me what this cryptic limerick means!

DORA. (*Though* OTHERS *try to stop her from telling him, waving their hands in briefly futile gestures as she begins:*) *I've* got it! (*Points.*) The smiling face is in that picture right behind you! (*Rushes to cord.*) And the cord is this long-unused bell-pull over here!

ROSALIND. Of all the lousy times to regain use of her brain!

MEDKINS. (*Who has looked at picture and cord while* DORA *spoke.*) Of course! That gold *frame*—it's *really* gold!

ORION. Imagine!

CLEO. All this time!

BARBARA. It's been right over our very noses!

BARNSY. Medkins—I mean, Barnaby—before you bump us all off—may I ask Barbara one question?

MEDKINS. Oh, all right, but hurry it up!

BARNSY. Barbara—when you first met the false Barnaby—I was wondering—

BARBARA. If *I* saw through his deception? Well, of *course* I did! Orion, I *told* you he used to study with me at Mrs. Michaels' amateur theatrical acting class, *didn't* I!

ORION. (*Much abashed.*) I must admit—she *did*!

BARBARA. It was that nice Mr. Tate Lawson. And I told you *that*, too! Dear me, now there'll be an opening in our class! (*Starts to rise.*) I must phone Mrs. Michaels—!

MEDKINS. Hold it! (*She sits.*) Now, there's nothing personal in this, but to cover my tracks, I really *must* bump you all off, and now!

BARNSY. But *why*, Barnaby?! Why have you *done* all this?!

MEDKINS. You don't know what it's like being the only pauper in a wealthy family! I had to scrounge for every bit of money I could get from you! It began to drive me mad! And then, when I heard Orion was about to cancel the tontine, with gold now selling for hundreds of dollars an ounce—I made up my mind! I'd been left *flat broke* so *many* times—I was *not* going to be left flat *again*! Now— (*Waves pistol.*) Shut your eyes!

CLEO. Just one moment!

ROSALIND. You asked before why we came back— well, there was a good reason.

MEDKINS. What reason?!

CLEO. We were stalling for time!

DORA. There, Jeff! I *told* you it was a good idea!

JEFF. Oh, be quiet, you idiot!

DORA. Well, if *that's* the way you feel, our engagement is *off*!

JEFF. Dora, *all* engagements are off! We're about to be *killed*!

ROSALIND. Not necessarily. You see—

CLEO. He no longer can spare the *time* to kill us!

MEDKINS. And why not?

ROSALIND. Because—the *police* are on the way!

CLEO. (*As* OTHERS *react suitably to their situation.*) After all, we were sitting in Barnsy's living room, *anyway*—so I thought—why not use her *phone*?

MEDKINS. Curses! Then I *have* no time! Dora— quickly—pull that cord!

JEFF. But Barnaby—

MEDKINS. Shut up! In another moment, I'll have over a million *pounds*!

DORA. (*Hand on bell-pull.*) Oh, nonsense. It can't *possibly* weigh more than a few *thousand*!

(*And just as* MEDKINS *realizes his peril,* DORA *blithely pulls the cord, and the picture topples downward toward* MEDKINS, *who crouches without even looking, hands atop his head, eyes scrunched shut, and*

*there is an abrupt LTB, during which* ALL BUT
MEDKINS *scream, and when LIGHTS COME UP,
he is gone [VCH], and the picture lies on its face
where he was just standing.*)

JEFF. (*Rushes to fallen picture.*) Quickly, help me get
it *off* of him!

(*He and whatever* OTHERS *can get to picture-edges grunt
and lift and tilt the picture back on its lower edge
against the hearth, then* ALL *look floorward* [*where
we cannot see*], *and* ALL BUT BARBARA *make faces
of ghastly revulsion and turn their backs, gagging,
as* BARBARA *calmly stoops and lifts a very flattened
"Medkins" into our view* [*this is a large cardboard
body, with a color-photo of your* MEDKINS—*player's
face—wearing an expression of horror, of course—
glued in the head-spot, which body the* MEDKINS-
*player in cubbyhole will slip to* BARBARA *before she
holds it up*].)

BARBARA. (*After the hilarious audience-response to
the sight.*) *Well*—we've left him flat *again*! (*Drops
figure, dusts off her hands.*)

JEFF. (*As* OTHERS *slowly calm down into normal state.*)
At last, the long nightmare is over—the sun will soon rise
again! (*INSTANT SUNLIGHT appears outside open
garden doors, and ROOM BRIGHTENS TO FULL IL-
LUMINATION.*) There, what'd I tell you! (*Rushes to*
CLEO, *embraces her.*) Darling, you saved us all!

DORA. What?! But *I* pulled the cord that *flattened*
him!

JEFF. But Cleo phoned the police, which is what rat-
tled him so badly that he *asked* you to pull it!

CLEO. Jeff—does this mean—you and I—together—
forever—?

JEFF. Why not!

CLEO. Gee, it's just like one of my *movies*! (*Flings her arms about his neck.*) Oh, Jeff, I love you so!

DORA. *I* love him, too!

CLEO. But I'm very rich, now!

DORA. Well, *I'm* very rich, too!

CLEO. And I'm a famous *movie* star!

DORA. (*Hesitates for half a beat as* OTHERS *look expectantly her way, then says to* BARBARA, *with resignation:*) You say there's an opening in your acting-class—?

(*Then* ALL *look toward kitchen-access in surprise as* MAGNOLIA *comes in, and overlap-adlib "Magnolia!", "Good heavens!", "But we thought—?!" and suchlike sentiments; then:*)

MAGNOLIA. What's the *matter* with all of you?

ORION. Damn and blast, girl--only a few hours ago, we saw you fall *dead*!

MAGNOLIA. Oh, that was only temporary.

ROSALIND. But you ate the *hors d'oeuvre* with the *poison* on it!

CLEO. So how can you be alive?!

MAGNOLIA. (*Shrugs prettily.*) I threw up.

(ALL *express relief—combined wry chuckles and sighs will do nicely here—then, as* JEFF *embraces* CLEO *and* ORION *embraces* ROSALIND *and a disconsolate* DORA *leans her head against* BARNSY'S *shoulder while* BARNSY *soothingly pats her on the back:*)

BARBARA. Do you know—I've just had the most comforting thought!

JEFF. After a night of total terror?

DORA. What *sort* of comforting thought, Aunt Barbara?

BARBARA. (*Beams radiantly out front, for:*) Why, that the *only* person who was brutally *murdered* tonight was merely an *actor*! (OTHERS *instantly do at "take" out front to the audience and then get looks of deep menace on their faces—after all,* they *are actors—and* slowly *start moving toward her, obviously primed to destroy;* BARBARA *abruptly realizes what she has just said, gets a sickly smile, and as they close in for the kill, she croaks in nervous desperation:*) *Let* me—re*phrase* that . . . !

(*But* OTHERS *are still closing in on her, with Death in their combined gazes, and she is cringing and awaiting her fate, as:*)

## THE CURTAIN FALLS

## SPECIAL INSTRUCTIONS

1) The "cubbyhole": Since the apparent upstage tablecloth-hanging is in reality the combined reflections of the left-and-right hangings, care should be taken that the cloth is stiff (so that persons who pass on left or right of cloth will not make it—and therefore the upstage reflection—flap or ripple); it should also not be even a little bit translucent, since shadows of passersby will also be seen moving along the reflection; however, an opaque cloth will cast the table-underside into deep shadow, and (since it is most important that the audience "see"—apparently—that there is nothing or no one under the table at any time) this means that the underside should be *lighted* as brightly as—or even slightly brighter than—the exterior stage area, either via a footlight-spot or a concealed bulb under the table itself. Needless to say, the table should be a large one, since the cubbyhole is only one-fourth of the tabletop-area, and must hide up to two persons in it at the same time.

2) The gold-framed portrait: This should be rigged so that, in its Act Three topple, it will first tilt out until it is parallel to the floor, pivoting on its bottom lip, and only then drop flatly down to—apparently—flatten the killer. The blackout at this point is merely so "Medkins" can scurry under the table as it drops, but if you want the scene visible, you might want to use strobe-lighting, so that the lightweight (it is suggested the "gold" frame be merely gilt-painted styrofoam) portrait will seem to move down upon the killer in split-second flashes of apparent massiveness; "Medkins," of course, much crouch *completely* from view before his scurry into the cubbyhole if you opt for this latter approach.

99

3) The cavalier-portrait slot: This should not "bag" between uses, obviously, so that the onstage characters will never see that there is a gap in the cloak-front at all. To achieve this, have the base of the forepart of the overlapped canvas secured (on the back-of-the-flat side, of course) with sturdy elastic, so that whenever that gloved hand withdraws, the cloak will snap flat again.

4) The parson's bench(es): The wall-segment that rotates 180 degrees should never over- or under-shoot complete "flushness' with the walls on either side of it when a rotation is completed. There are two different ways to accomplish this: A) Have the casters or wheels supporting the circular platform set on a track which "*peaks*" at the 90-degree position, and "*bottoms*" at the full-turn position; in this way, once its passes the 90-degree mark, it will roll snugly into its stop-position gravitationally. However, this approach is more difficult (building the peaked-and-bottomed track correctly is a real engineering feat) than B) Always rotate the platform in the same direction (counterclockwise is preferred, since the audience will tend to try and keep the *disappearing* bench in view rather than look for the companion-bench to appear, and hence are less likely to look through the temporary gap and see the interior of the "dark passageway beyond" in any memorable detail, which will save you a lot of work making that interior looking solidly authentic), and have a pivoted "Stop" (a short length of two-by-four that can pivot from a vertical to a horizontal position will do the trick) on the back of the flat: Lift this prior to a rotation, and drop it as the rotation becomes complete, to stop the moving wall-segment.

5) Lights: It is worth repeating again—since it is most vital—that during any blackout, *total* darkness is essential. The fireplace, chandeliers, and table-underlight must *all* go black each time the stage-lighting does, or the "magical disappearance/appearance" is lost, and with it a lot of the show's visual fun.

# LIST OF PROPERTIES

*ACT ONE*

Preset: tray, stemglasses, full sherry decanter on sideboard; container of long wooden matches at hearth; dusty stationery in desk drawer; in another desk drawer, so that JEFF and DORA can hold each item aloft as they name it, are a bottle of ink, a stapler, a ruler, a box of rubberbands, an eraser, a paperweight, and a wooden pencil (pre-cut through wood but not through graphite so that it will snap properly in two); a stagehand in cubbyhole to take the poisoned drink during blackout, and to assist BARNABY in switching from his jacket to one with a dagger-handle (and bloodstains, if you like) immovably attached between the shoulderblades so it won't come off when JEFF and/or DORA contact it during death scene.

MAGNOLIA: featherduster at top of show; tray of hors d'oeuvre from kitchen; pair of suitcases from front hall (by the way, you need only use two suitcases in the entire show—simply have her hand them to prop person after each exit upstairs, and take them back after each return to front hall—and after JEFF and BARNABY take them upstairs, they can be handed to prop person who will give them to DORA for her entrance; if these bags are eminently recognizable as the same pair [with, say, prominent travel-stickers, bizarre colors, etc.], so much the more fun for your audience)

MEDKINS: evening newspaper from front hall

DORA: topcoat and suitcases [see above] for entrance from garden

KILLER'S HAND: vial of green poison behind cavalier portrait

CLEO: her dress should have a pocket, for her reference to same after she reappears in Act Two; it should also be easily removable, since she must reappear without it from cubbyhole in Act Two

BARNSY: a chain about her neck with her jambule on it till after her vanishment-and-return in Act Two

101

*ACT TWO*

Clear: Dora's coat/bags; tray of hors d'oeuvre; used glasses; and, of course, Barnaby

Preset: refill sherry decanter; fresh glasses on sideboard; close the garden doors

Orion: bonds and gag for his reappearance on bench from wall

Killer's Hand: vial of green poison behind cavalier portrait; pistol (loaded with blanks) in same place for gunshot

Dora: charm bracelet *after* she goes upstairs and returns with others; jambule on it must have rolled paper in it for her to remove

Magnolia: broom from kitchen

*ACT THREE*

Clear: used glasses; Magnolia's body; broom

Preset: refill sherry decanter; fresh glasses on sideboard; open garden doors; bowl of marshmallows on table; have Side #2 of bench in view; put stationery and pencil-half on desktop for Cleo to take and use; and whatever you do, don't forget your cardboard Medkins in the cubbyhole!

Jeff: pistol on person from top of act; bonds and loosened gag for his re-entrance via cellar archway

Barbara: lurid-covered mystery magazine at top of act

Dora: pre-toasted marshmallow on stick at top of act; charm bracelet with jambule on wrist

Cleo: a new dress, suitcases, for her entrance down the stairs; a ragged duplicate of this dress for her re-entrance from garden

Rosalind: ragged duplicate of her dress, also, for return with Cleo

Medkins: pistol in hand for his rotation into room on bench; jambule in his pocket to palm and pretend to take from Barbara's ear, with rolled paper inside it

SOUND EFFECTS: sonorous door chimes; very loud thunderclaps

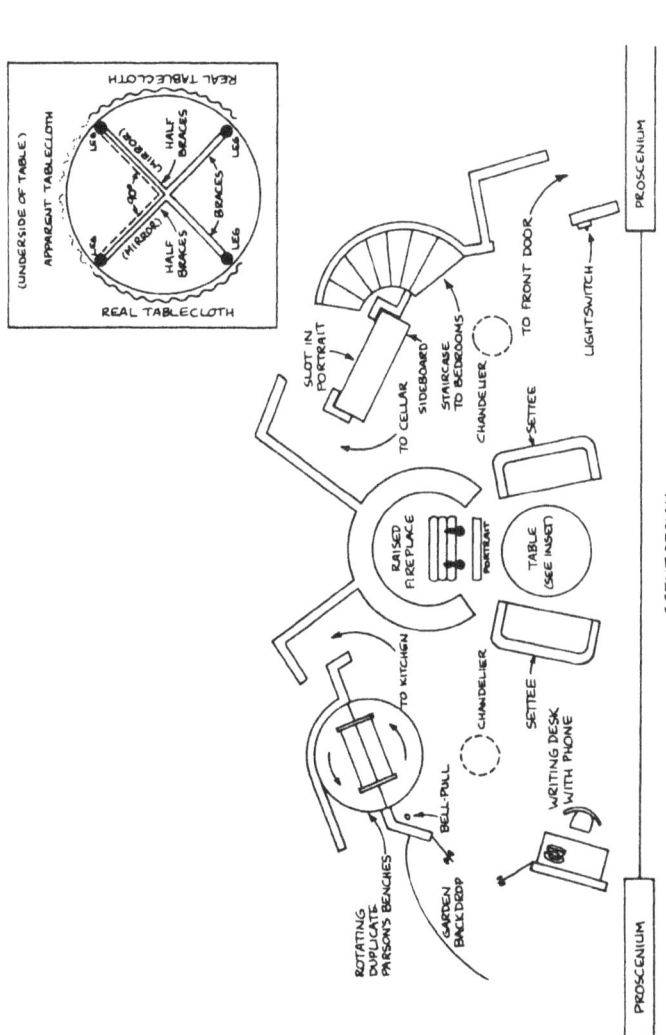

SCENE DESIGN

"BUT WHY BUMP OFF BARNABY?"

Ingram Content Group UK Ltd.
Milton Keynes UK
UKHW020700240723
425668UK00014B/641